PURRFECT BABY

THE MYSTERIES OF MAX 49

NIC SAINT

PURRFECT BABY

The Mysteries of Max 49

Copyright © 2021 by Nic Saint

All rights reserved. No part of this book may be reproduced in any form by any electronic or mechanical means including photocopying, recording, or information storage and retrieval without permission in writing from the author.

This is a work of fiction. Names, characters, places, brands, media, and incidents are either the product of the author's imagination or are used fictitiously. The author acknowledges the trademarked status and trademark owners of various products referenced in this work of fiction, which have been used without permission. The publication/use of these trademarks is not authorized, associated with, or sponsored by the trademark owners.

Edited by Chereese Graves

www.nicsaint.com

Give feedback on the book at: info@nicsaint.com

facebook.com/nicsaintauthor
@nicsaintauthor

First Edition

Printed in the U.S.A

PURRFECT BABY

New Kitten on the Block

The day had finally arrived when Odelia was about to give birth to a new member of the family. Unfortunately the day had also arrived that Gran decided to adopt a dog and gift him to Chase. And if that wasn't bad enough, two murders took place that Odelia, in her highly pregnant state, and in spite of everyone's protestations, felt compelled to investigate.

The owner of an escort service had been found murdered, and so had one of her escorts. It soon became clear that they'd been engaged in a unique service that offered wives and fiancées the possibility to have their husbands and fiancés put to the ultimate fidelity test. And since their service had been very successful, there were suspects galore: was it one of those same fiancés or husbands, trying to stop their fling from coming to light, or was it a cheated partner looking for revenge? Suffice it to say, we had our work cut out for us.

CHAPTER 1

*D*otty Berg relaxed in front of the vanity mirror and started removing her makeup. She wasn't usually the kind of girl who liked to use excessive makeup but in her line of work it was unfortunately a given that she should. In spite of the fact that tonight had been a success she felt bone-tired. Calista would be pleased—the client perhaps less so, even though she'd gotten them the results they paid for. But that wasn't her fault now was it?

She mechanically removed the last remnants of eyeliner from her eyes and for a moment gazed at her reflection in the mirror. A remarkably fresh-faced young woman stared back at her. Remarkable because she'd done this job for so long now she had become a little world-weary. But fortunately that hadn't yet had an effect on her good looks. And nor it should. The moment she started being affected by the turmoil that her chosen profession inevitably brought with it, she'd quit. That's what she had always told Calista and that's how it would be. Then again—the work did pay shockingly well.

She checked her phone for messages and repaired to the

bed, prepared to get ready for the night. It had gotten later than she thought, the client requiring a lot of patient hand-holding and encouragement but finally she'd gotten him exactly where she wanted him. It was a skill set not easily acquired but one she was nevertheless proud of.

And as she stretched out languorously on top of the duvet, she thought she heard a sound from the modest little hallway. Had she forgotten to close the door? It was entirely possible. These last couple of days had been challenging, and sometimes she didn't know where her head was at.

With a tired groan, she sat up and swung her feet from the bed. Hugging her pink satin dressing gown around herself, she shuffled over to have a look. Moments later, she was staggering back into her bedroom, grabbing for her phone. And she'd just started typing a message of distress to Calista when the phone was unceremoniously snatched from her trembling fingers and she was pushed back on the bed. And as he straddled her, she knew that this time she'd gone too far.

§

Calista Dunne had drifted off to sleep on the couch, a glass of Pinot Noir still in her hand, the TV blaring away and providing the background sound to a pretty sweet dream. In her dream she was relaxing poolside in Mallorca. The sun was warm on her skin, the clear blue water from the pool lapping pleasantly at her feet, the cares of the world a million miles away.

She woke up and automatically grabbed for her phone to see if her husband had left her any messages. He was away on business so she had the house to herself. She yawned until she caught the odd message Dotty had sent. 'He's come back —you've got to—'

"Got to what?" she murmured as she blinked, bleary-eyed, at the message.

She immediately placed the phone to her ear and waited for Dotty to pick up. But Dotty didn't pick up. The special app they used to keep in touch just kept on ringing and ringing to no avail.

She pursed her lips and chewed the inside of her bottom lip, a habit she was trying to break since it could only lead to premature wrinklage.

He's come back. That could mean two things, and in both cases it was probably bad news. Or why else would Dotty feel the need to send her a message at this late hour?

For a few moments she felt irresolute, and she'd already decided to head over there to stave off disaster, when her phone buzzed. It was Dotty again: 'It's fine. He forgot his wallet. Hope I didn't wake you.' Smiley face, smiley face, smiley face, heart emoji.

She smiled and relaxed. False alarm. Still. That self-defense training she'd signed her girls up for was starting to feel like a better idea every day. Maybe even shooting lessons.

She splashed some more of the Pinot into her glass—keep that nice buzz going—and sank back down on the couch.

Moments later, she was fast asleep, and only woke up when he was already straddling her, tying a nylon stocking around her neck and pulling—hard.

CHAPTER 2

Vesta Muffin didn't often visit the shelter that carried her name, even though she knew she probably should. When her son had opened it along with his girlfriend Charlene Butterwick, the town's mayor, she'd even promised to volunteer there, but that had never materialized of course. In her defense, she was a busy woman, and her time was probably better spent elsewhere. And besides, the Vesta Muffin Animal Shelter had a perfectly capable manager now taking care of things. Marsella Horowicz had been handpicked by Charlene to run the shelter and by all accounts she was doing a great job of it.

The shelter itself still looked new and clean, contrary to the pound that had existed before, and which had been an abomination and a thorn in the side of every animal lover in town. At the new shelter the animals were well taken care of by a small contingent of volunteers who didn't stint in their affection for the creatures who were forced to spend time there, whether short or long, depending how quickly new homes could be found.

Vesta had decided to pay a visit to the shelter with her new boyfriend Dallas de Pravé, a wealthy businessman and investor she'd met on her recent Norwegian cruise. He was Finnish, as far as she knew, and as rich as the sea in those Norwegian fjords was deep. And so if there was anyone who could invest in the shelter it was definitely Dallas.

The billionaire - tan, stocky, handsome and about Vesta's own age - was bobbing his head with distinct interest as Marsella showed them around the facility.

"So how long does it usually take you to find a new home for your darlings?" Vesta wanted to know.

"Days, sometimes. Weeks at the most."

"That's good," said Vesta as she stared at a particularly moody-looking mutt who stared back at her as if to say: 'So what's your problem then, sweetheart?'

Marsella, who was fortyish and very efficient but also very blond and blue-eyed, was standing a little too close to Dallas to Vesta's liking, so she inserted herself between the two, even as Dallas pointed to a tiny doggie and said, "What he?"

"That's a Brussels Griffon," said Marsella. "Her name is Windex."

"Windex?" asked Vesta with a frown. "What kind of a name is that?"

"It's the name her previous owner gave her."

"What was he? A window washer?"

"No, she was an elderly lady who had to move into a nursing home where unfortunately they don't allow pets. And since her daughter wasn't interested in providing a home for Windex she was forced to put her up with us until we can find her a suitable new pet parent." She gave Vesta a gentle smile. "Want to hold her for a moment?"

"Oh, no," said Vesta, waving a hand. "I know what you're

trying to do, and you have to cut that out right now. My home is full. Four cats is more than enough for any person."

"Win-dex," Dallas murmured, enunciating carefully. "Win... dex."

"You can take her, if you want," said Vesta. "You like dogs? Dallas?"

"Mh?" said the aged billionaire.

"Do you like dogs?" she repeated, gesticulating extensively.

"Yes, yes," he murmured with a smile. "Windex dog."

"He doesn't speak English?" asked Marsella.

"He's Finnish," Vesta explained.

"How did you meet?"

"Aboard a cruise ship in Norway. I told him my name was Vesta Muffin and he said 'I like American muffin' and we never looked back. So how long has Windex been here?"

"Three weeks, and she's really pining, I can tell. It's heartbreaking, really."

"It is," Vesta agreed as she took in the poor little creature that was staring at her with its liquid brown eyes, as if imploring her to do something. "Why is no one taking her?"

"I don't know. She looks a little funny, so kids tend not to like her and adults think she's probably too set in her ways after having spent so many years with the same person. I try to tell them she's the sweetest thing on earth but they just look at her and shiver."

Vesta frowned. "Why? She looks fine to me."

Marsella dropped her voice and whispered into Vesta's ear, "They say she looks like a bat."

Vesta studied the tiny doggie some more. Windex did look a little like a bat, with her big ears and her small snout. Even the coloring was a little bat-like. "So?" she said. "Kids love those Batman movies. You could tell them Windex is Batman's little helper."

Marsella laughed. "Now there's an idea."

"Win-dex," Dallas said slowly. "Dog." He smiled. "Windex, dog."

"Yes, yes, Windex is a dog," said Vesta impatiently. The man might be made of money but he was definitely an odd bird. "Okay, fine," she said, making one of her trademark swift decisions. "I'll take her. Did she get all her shots and stuff?"

Marsella stared at her. "You'll take her?"

"Sure, why not? She looks like a sweet little thing, and my grandson-in-law loves dogs."

"Absolutely," said Marsella, and pressed a warm hand upon Vesta's arm. "You won't be sorry."

"I'm not so sure about that," Vesta murmured as she followed Marsella to the office.

Behind them, Dallas trailed. "Windex dog," he was muttering.

In the office she met one of the volunteers: Shelley Eccleston looked like a teenager but was probably older than she looked. Then again, all young people looked like teenagers to Vesta, with their unblemished faces and their peach-perfect skin.

"Can you prepare the paperwork for Windex, Shelley?" asked Marsella. "Vesta is taking her home."

"Ooh, that's great!" said the girl with all the fervor of youth. "You're a saint, Mrs. Muffin. An absolute saint."

"Yeah, yeah, yeah," said Vesta as she watched Dallas stare at Shelley, open-mouthed as if he'd never seen a pretty girl before. "Better close that trap or you'll catch flies," she told him, but of course he didn't understand a word she said. She was starting to regret bringing this particular billionaire home with her. Tough to communicate if he only spoke Finnish—or at least that's what she assumed those garbled guttural tones that sometimes fell from his tongue when he talked into his phone were—and she only spoke English.

She'd hoped the language of love would see them through but there had been none of that either. At first she'd thought he was simply shy, but now she was starting to think he was one of those eunuchs. Or was it unicorns? She never knew which was which.

At least he wasn't married—or at least she didn't think he was. No mention of a Mrs. Dallas de Pravé had ever been made, and when she googled the guy she hadn't found any evidence of a marital entanglement either. Like her, he was widowed with two kids, both now already with kids themselves. All of them had funny names like Jarmo and Eeto and Arvo and reportedly the de Pravés were amongst the richest families in Finland.

A young kid walked in, looking as youthful and fresh-faced as Shelley, and the latter said, "Can you get Windex ready, Gavin? Mrs. Muffin is taking her home with her."

The kid stared at her. "Mrs. Muffin?" he said finally. "Vesta Muffin?"

"That's my name—don't wear it out," she quipped.

The kid's eyes swiveled from her to the picture of her that hung next to the 'Vesta Muffin Animal Shelter' sign behind the counter and he blinked, then a smile spread across his freckled face. "It's an honor, Mrs. Muffin. You did a great thing starting this shelter."

She would have told the kid who was probably all of nineteen that she hadn't exactly started the shelter, merely given her name to it, but who was she to deprive this young man of this honest pleasure. "I feel it's important we all do what we can to give our furry little friends a better life... Gavin, is it?"

He nodded fervently. "Gavin Blemish. And you're absolutely right, Mrs. Muffin."

"Blemish, as in Garwen Blemish?"

"Yeah, he's my dad."

"I always buy my shoes there. Great place."

"Best place in town," he said, and flashed her a toothy smile. Perfect white teeth, of course, she couldn't help but notice with a small measure of chagrin. "Next time you come in I'll make sure you get a discount, Mrs. Muffin."

"Oh, so you work there, do you?"

"Yeah, I'm only volunteering here," he said with a slight diminution of happiness. "Though I'd love to work here full-time," he added, eyeing her with a look of hope as if she was made of money and he wouldn't mind having some. "I absolutely adore our animals."

"Uh-huh. More than shoes, you mean?"

"Oh, absolutely. I mean, shoes are fine, but animals—well, they need us, don't they?"

"Same here," said Shelley.

"So where do you work, Shelley?" asked Vesta, who wondered if these two were boyfriend and girlfriend. They looked as if they might be.

"I work for my dad, actually. He runs Eccleston Concrete. It's a cement factory," she explained. "I work in the office. But I spend as much time here at your shelter as I can."

She would have dissuaded them from the notion that she actually owned the shelter but they were both gazing at her with such abject admiration that she didn't have the heart. "Well, you're both doing a great job here," she said. "And I can only thank you and tell you to keep up the good work."

She glanced over to Dallas, who was now eyeing a chart that offered an overview of the different species of dogs that are out there, and was mouthing their names to himself. If she ever managed to talk to the guy, and convince him to invest in the shelter, maybe Marsella could offer both Shelley and Gavin an actual contract.

Then again, who was she kidding? She'd seen the numbers. There simply wasn't enough work for three full-timers. So she merely smiled encouragingly at the two young people and watched them return to work—getting little Windex ready for his new home.

CHAPTER 3

Once Vesta and her companion had left, the warm sensation of accomplishment that had briefly swept through Marsella quickly dissipated, and the cloud of dread that had been hanging over her all week made a sudden comeback, like it always did. Gavin had gone to clean out the gerbil cages and now it was just Marsella and Shelley.

Shelley must have noticed something, for she suddenly said, "Is everything all right?"

She could have lied and told her everything was fine, but Shelley was no fool. Plus, in the months they'd known each other they'd become great friends. Which was odd, since she could have been Shelley's mom, but Shelley was such a warmhearted person and so easy to talk to it wasn't hard to see why she'd become increasingly fond of the young woman.

She finally sighed and slumped against the counter. "It's Dewey. Yet another one of his old girlfriends came crawling out of the woodwork last week to warn me about him."

"Not again," said Shelley, her expression a vivid tableau of compassion.

Marsella nodded. "On Facebook this time. Sent me a friend request and a message out of the blue. Said she'd heard about the wedding and wanted me to know what kind of a man Dewey Toneu really is. Then if I still wanted to marry him at least I'd know what I was letting myself in for."

"Did you tell Dewey?"

She shook her head. "Not yet."

"How long ago was the affair?"

"Um, about... three years ago maybe? Apparently he was juggling five different girlfriends at the time, and they all accidentally found out about each other when Dewey sent a group email to all of them and forgot to put them in BCC. They actually got together one night and discovered he'd promised all of them he'd marry them. Or so she says, this Mary-Lynn." She was trying hard to keep the bitterness and anxiousness out of her voice but judging from the look on Shelley's face she wasn't doing a particularly good job.

"You have to talk to Dewey, Marsella."

"I did talk to him, when the first of his exes got in touch. He admitted dating her, but said that he'd been a different person back then." She gave Shelley a hesitant look. "He says that none of those girls meant anything to him. That I'm the only one for him now. *The* one. That the moment we met he knew his old life of casual dating was finally over."

"He could be right. Three years is a long time. He's probably older and wiser now."

"You think?"

"Has any of these girls dated him since you met?"

"No. Mary-Lynn was three years ago, and the other one, um... Francine—four years."

"See? I'm sure that if Dewey was cheating on you, you'd know. It's hard to keep this stuff secret in this day and age of social media."

"Yeah, but if he really was dating some other girl she

wouldn't tell me, would she? She'd simply hope the wedding doesn't go through. Or maybe she's one of those girls who don't mind dating a married man—even prefers it, for the lack of attachment."

"Look, if you really wanted to be sure, you'd almost have to hire a private detective. Have Dewey followed around the clock to see if he's as committed to you as he says he is."

She gave the girl a keen look.

"Oh, no, you didn't," said Shelley, clearly shocked.

"No, I didn't," she admitted. "But I have considered it."

"Well, maybe you should. Just to put your mind at ease."

"It's just that... he's such a catch, you know. It's very hard to date a man who's as attractive and as successful as Dewey. A lot of insecurities suddenly start to pop up."

"Hey, don't sell yourself short, Marsella," said Shelley, giving her a gentle nudge. "You're quite a catch yourself, you know. In fact it's Dewey who should be worried, not you."

She smiled and felt her mood lift. "You always know what to say to make me feel better, don't you?"

"Then it's a good thing you made me your maid of honor."

Just then, a family with two little girls walked into the office, and work beckoned, cutting their conversation short. But as she escorted the family out to take a look at the kennels, she found herself revisiting the idea of hiring a private detective. If it offered her peace of mind, why not? And so she decided to check listings for PIs in the area tonight.

CHAPTER 4

It had been a particularly lazy morning for us. Odelia and Chase had both left and gone to work, and for once all four of us had opted to stay home and relax instead. Lately Odelia hadn't stepped out of the office much, since she was about to give birth any moment now, and so Dan had figured it was unwise for her to go out and interview people until after she'd delivered the baby. Odelia's opinion in the matter was different, of course: she wanted to keep busy right up until the last possible moment, and her doctor hadn't given her any indication why she couldn't, which strengthened her in her view.

But with nothing much going on at the paper, and nothing going on at the police station, Dooley, Brutus, Harriet and myself had figured we should take advantage of these final days or weeks before the big change was upon us: the arrival of the new baby.

"So do you think it's going to be a boy or a girl?" asked Dooley, not for the first time.

"I don't know, Dooley, and Odelia isn't telling, so speculation is pointless."

"But why, Max? Why aren't they telling us? We have a right to know."

"Not really," I said. "And besides, maybe they don't know themselves."

"I think they know," said Harriet. "And they're simply not telling anyone."

"But why!" Dooley insisted. "We have to know, so we can prepare ourselves."

"What difference does it make?" I said. "Babies are babies, whatever their gender."

"That's where you're wrong, Max," said Brutus. "There's a huge difference."

"Of course there is," I said, yawning and hoping everyone would shut up so I could get some nap time in. Why else had we stayed home if not to enjoy some peace and quiet while we still could?

"Boys are much more rambunctious," said Brutus. "Girls are quieter. So my vote is for a girl."

"It's not an election, sweetie," said Harriet. "We don't get to vote."

"I know, but if we could vote, I'd choose a girl. So fingers crossed."

"You don't even have fingers," I pointed out.

"I think it's going to be a girl," said Dooley.

"What makes you say that?" said Brutus.

"One of your silly documentaries again?" said Harriet.

"They're not silly, and for your information I read about this on the internet. You can see from the shape of the belly whether it's going to be a boy or a girl, and I'm almost one hundred percent sure Odelia's belly is a girl belly. It's more… oval? More round, you know."

I didn't know, and frankly I didn't care. Babies are pretty much all the same in my experience: small and loud and annoying. I just hoped they'd get it over with and bring it home already. And if it did prove to be too much for us, we could always move next door and spend the formative years of the child's life with Marge and Tex.

"How long does it take for a baby to become less of a nuisance?" I asked.

"Years," said Brutus.

"Years?" It wasn't the answer I'd hoped for. "I thought months."

"Oh, no. They only develop into actual human beings when they get their first job and strike out on their own, which is probably when they turn twenty-four, maybe twenty-three if you're lucky. If they can't land a decent job they can't move into their own place and then you're stuck with them pretty much indefinitely. In fact Tigger was telling us the other day that his human's daughter is still living with them, even though she's thirty."

"Thirty!"

"Can you imagine?"

"Thirty years of diapers," said Dooley knowingly.

"I don't think kids wear diapers until they're thirty," said Harriet. "Probably they grow out of the habit much sooner."

"Some kids are fine," said Brutus. "Tigger's human's daughter is all right and she has been all right for a long time. Doesn't scream or shout or make his life miserable. In fact she's the one who feeds him now and even cleans out his litter box. But they tell me that's rare. Most kids refuse to do anything around the home. They just sort of mope around."

We all looked appropriately impressed. "Tigger is lucky," I said finally.

"It's a lottery," said Brutus, repeating a universal truth we'd heard from many sources. "Either you end up with some pocket psychopath who likes to pull tails and poke eyes, or you end up with Tigger's human's daughter, who's a very normal, very nice person."

"Which is why we need to pray Odelia has a girl, you guys," said Dooley. "Because we all know that girls are nice and boys are hellraisers who'll make our lives miserable."

And as the discussion raged on, I decided to tune them all out and catch up on my nap time. Whether Odelia had a girl or a boy, at least that way I was way ahead of the curve.

Just then, the sliding glass door slid back and Gran walked in. That strange billionaire fiancé she's been hanging out with lately wasn't with her this time. The man hadn't exchanged one intelligible word with any of the rest of the family, and all he seemed to do was follow Gran around everywhere, a sort of perpetual smile on his face. He seemed nice enough, but it would be even nicer if he decided to give us the benefit of his conversation.

"Where is everyone?" asked Gran.

"Work," I said as I adjusted my position on the couch.

And that's when I saw it.

A dog. In Gran's arms.

"What's that, Gran?" asked Dooley, who'd noticed the same curious phenomenon.

"What do you think it is? A dog, of course. Okay, so I'm just going to leave her here," she said, and deposited the small bundle of fur on the couch right next to us!

"Gran, what are you doing!" Harriet cried as she jumped up from her position.

"Oh, don't get your knickers in a twist," said Gran irritably. "It's just a dog."

"But... whose dog is it?" asked Brutus, eyeing the creature suspiciously.

"Chase's dog, of course. Though he doesn't know it yet."

"Chase's dog!" Brutus cried. "But Chase already has a pet. Me!"

"Well, so now he's got another one. And besides, Chase always wanted a dog."

"But Gran!" Harriet practically wailed.

Gran held up her hand. "No need to thank me. You're welcome."

And with these words, she strode out again. Then, as if she'd just remembered, she opened the door a crack and said, "Oh, her name is Windex, by the way." And was gone.

CHAPTER 5

We all stared at the little dog. Though at the moment it was hard to know whether it actually was a dog. We only had Gran's word for it. It looked more like... a bat. It had big bat ears, and big bat eyes that stared at us piteously, and a small almost hairless body.

"What are you?" asked Harriet finally.

"Are you going to eat me?" asked the doggie, looking at the four of us with abject fear written all over its features. And I could imagine what it was thinking: being dumped on a couch with four big cats hovering over it, staring it down. Not a fun welcome!

So I decided to do the right thing and held out my paw. "My name is Max," I said. "Welcome to the Pooles." Though in actual fact I should have said the Kingsleys, of course. Hard to get used to such a minor thing as a name change.

The doggie watched the approach of my paw and produced a sort of panicky yelp then attempted to jump down from the couch and get as far away from me as possible!

Now I am a big boy, of course, and probably dwarfed this creature several times, but this was simply taking things too far. "I won't hurt you," I assured the batlike thing.

"Max may look like a bruiser," said Brutus, "but he's just a big softie. Me, on the other hand," he continued, pushing out his chest, "am a bruiser, but you'll find that I'm a nice bruiser. A bruiser who takes care of his own. A bruiser, in other words, who's one of the good guys."

The little doggie wasn't convinced, though, and was still measuring the distance to the floor and contemplating ways and means to escape from this dreadful place.

"And my name is Harriet," said Harriet. "Like Max, I'm a big softie, and I'm also a great friend of dogs. Two of my best friends are dogs, actually. Rufus and Fifi. I don't know if you've met them? They live next door and they're very nice. For dogs, I mean." And she plastered an ingratiating smile onto her face, hoping to impress it upon this newcomer that we were a dog-friendly environment and there was nothing to be scared of.

Her heartfelt appeal failed to grip, though, and the dog continued her escape attempts.

"I'm Dooley," said Dooley. "Are you a bat, Windex? Cause you look like a bat. So are you a bat? If you are, that's fine. I've never met a bat before. Can you fly?"

The doggie now paused from its endeavors and fixed Dooley with a curious look. "Why would you think I'm a bat, cat?"

"Because you look like a bat," Dooley said. "Only I can't see your wings, so now I'm thinking you're probably a bat that doesn't fly. So how do you get around? And is it true that you live in a cave and only come out at night? Do you sleep hanging upside down?"

The doggie now produced a sort of diffident smile. "You're pulling my leg, aren't you?"

Dooley shook his head. "Why would I want to pull your leg? Do you even have legs? Oh, you do. That's great. So you're a bat with no wings but with legs. Which makes you a very special kind of bat." Then his eyes widened. "Oh! I know! You're Batman!"

"I'm not Batman," said Windex. "I'm a dog. In fact I'm a Brussels Griffon."

Dooley frowned. "You don't look like a dog."

"Well, I can assure you that I am a dog." He studied Dooley for a moment. "You know? You're like no cat I have ever met. You're... weird."

"Gee, thanks," said Dooley happily. "You're also weird, Windex."

The doggie produced a grin as he took us all in. "If I'd known this was a cat household I'd have told that old lady I'd pass. But maybe you guys are not as bad as you look."

"What do you mean?" asked Harriet prissily. "We all look wonderful. Though I look a little more wonderful than the others, of course, but that's because I was born this way."

"So Windex," I said, "have you come here to stay?"

She shrugged. "I'm not sure. I used to belong to Eileen Dobson, but Eileen moved into a place where they don't like pets, and so I was sent to this place where they collect pets that aren't wanted anymore. And then some old lady showed up with an orange guy in tow and said she'd adopt me. And now all of a sudden I'm here with you guys. So am I staying or am I going? Honestly I don't know anymore. It's all very confusing. But what I will tell you is that I'm pretty tired of being shuffled around all the time."

"So your human didn't want you anymore?" asked Dooley. "That's so sad."

"Oh, she wanted me plenty, but the place where they took her doesn't care about pets."

"You're lucky, cause this place loves pets," said Dooley. "In fact they adore them. Though mostly cats, not bats. But I'm sure that in time they'll learn to love bats, too."

"He's not a bat, Dooley," said Harriet. "He's a dog."

"And I'm not a he but a she," said Windex.

"Oh," said Dooley as he tried to wrap his mind around this. "We're having a baby soon," he announced.

Windex frowned at this. "You're having kittens? But I thought you were a he, not a she?" Then he glanced to Harriet. "Oh, you mean you're having kittens? Congratulations."

Harriet's face morphed into a perfect pout. "Please don't mention the K word, dog."

"What did I say?"

"It's a touchy subject," said Brutus. Then he lowered his voice. "We've all been neutered," he whispered.

"So who's having the baby?"

"Odelia," said Dooley. "And so we're getting ready to move next door for the next thirty years, unless the baby is a girl, in which case we might stay here, if she proves to be nice."

"I'm sure the baby will be nice enough," I told my friend.

Though to be absolutely honest, I wasn't sure if Odelia would be thrilled to find a dog on her couch when she arrived home later today. As if four cats wasn't enough to contend with, now she'd have to take care of another pet. Timing is everything in these matters, you see. When parents suddenly show up with a puppy, their kids most likely will be over the moon. When an aged grandparent foists a quirky-looking dog on her pregnant granddaughter, her response might not be as exuberant as she would have hoped.

And just when relations between the natives of the Kingsley home and this relative newcomer were starting to thaw a little, Odelia suddenly came storming in, clutching her phone and looking a little feverish. "Let's go, you guys," she said. "There's been a murder!"

CHAPTER 6

We arrived at the apartment block in Chase's car. Odelia preferred to be driven around everywhere these days, as she had a little trouble squeezing behind the wheel of her own aged pickup. And Chase actually preferred to be his pregnant wife's chauffeur, driving at a snail's pace and braking well in advance of any crossroads and generally being the most careful driver the world has ever seen, much to Odelia's annoyance, actually. She likes to keep up a good pace, and to get from point A to point B in an expedient way.

"So what have we got?" asked Odelia as Chase helped her out of the car.

"Dotty Ludkin," said Chase, "though she also went by the name Dotty Berg, apparently. Her dad called it in. He was meeting her first thing this morning, and when she didn't open the door, he let himself in and found her."

"He had a spare key?"

"Yeah, he did."

We all glanced up at the building. It was tall and sported at least ten floors. "So where does she live, this Dotty Ludkin or Berg?" asked Odelia as she blew a strand of hair from her face.

"Top floor," said Chase.

She gave him a pleading look. "Elevator?" And when he nodded, she smiled.

Dotty Berg, as apparently she liked to be known, was lying on a bed in the middle of a nicely appointed room. There were lots of fabrics: not only plenty of carpets spread out across her apartment but also wall tapestries, curtains of different length and color, and throw pillows everywhere you looked. All in all it lent the apartment, and especially the bedroom, a certain atmosphere that reminded me of... a house of ill repute somehow.

Abe Cornwall, the county coroner, stood bent over the dead woman, examining her closely. When we walked in, he straightened.

"So what have you got for us, Abe?" asked Chase.

"Dead girl, late twenties, strangled to death with a nylon stocking. Other stocking seems to have gone missing."

"When did she die?"

"Some time last night, I'd say. Between midnight and two o'clock."

"So cause of death was strangulation?"

"I'd say so. No other injuries as far as I can tell at first glance. Some bruising on her upper arms so she was probably pinned down on the bed while being strangled."

"Fingernails?"

He shook his head, indicating her fingernails were intact and clean, so if she fought against her assailant, she hadn't been able to claw at their face or clothes so there would be no trace evidence found there. "I'll know more once I've taken a closer look," he said.

And since Abe's people were busy collecting evidence, we repaired to the hallway, where we encountered one of

Chase's plainclothes colleagues, Sarah Flunk. "Strangest thing, sir," said Sarah. "We found no phone or laptop on the scene."

"The killer probably took them," said Chase, nodding.

"She was known under two different names?" asked Odelia.

"Yes, the name on the bell is Dotty Ludkin, her official name, but we spoke to the neighbors, and one of them once heard her use the name Dotty Berg, which seems to be an assumed name. Oh, and this same neighbor said she heard a big argument yesterday coming from the apartment. She lives right underneath here, and says she almost called the police."

"We better have a chat with the neighbor," said Chase. "Dotty's dad found her?"

"Yes, we've got him downstairs in a car. He's really shaken up."

"Let's talk to him first, and then the neighbor," said Chase.

"Oh, and her dad said she works for a caterer, only we called the caterer and he says she didn't work there anymore. Hadn't worked there for the past ten months."

"Better knock on some more doors," said Chase. "In fact cover the entire street. Ask if they saw anyone leave the apartment last night. Abe puts time of death between midnight and two, so—"

"I'll take care of it, sir," said Sarah, who had done this kind of thing before many times.

"And if you need more people, just say the word and I'll talk to the Chief."

Sydney Ludkin had indeed taken his daughter's death very hard. He was a big man with coarse features but he now sat slumped in one of the police vans, sipping from a cup of coffee a kindly officer had brought him, and looking wan and pale. He looked up when we entered the van, and didn't even seem surprised to see Chase being accompanied by a very pregnant woman and two cats, such was his distress.

"I'm sorry to have to do this at this time, sir," said Chase as he took a seat across from the man in the back of the van, which had been outfitted with a desk and benches for this exact purpose, "but I would like to ask you a few questions if I may. You had arranged to meet Dotty this morning?"

Mr. Ludkin nodded and rubbed his cheek. "She'd asked me to take a look at her heater. It was acting up again, and since the owner couldn't be bothered, I thought I'd take a look before we called in a professional, which would run into money. I rang the bell and knocked, but when she didn't answer, I let myself in with the key and... and..." His voice broke and it took a little time to collect himself again. "I... found her."

"Do you have any idea who might have done this to Dotty, sir?" asked Odelia kindly.

The man shook his head. "No idea whatsoever. Dotty was the sweetest girl. I just don't get it."

"The door wasn't open? Lock forced or anything?" asked Chase.

"No, the door was closed when I arrived."

"You didn't notice anything out of the ordinary? No signs of a break-in?"

"No, everything looked fine to me. Dotty keeps her apartment clean. She hates mess."

"She used to work for a caterer?"

"Still does, as far as I know."

"We called the caterer, and they told us she stopped working for them ten months ago."

The man frowned. "Ten months ago? She never said anything about that."

"As far as you're aware she was still working there?"

"Yeah, of course. There must be some mistake. When she called me on the phone yesterday she said they were catering some big wedding next weekend and her feet were already hurting just thinking about it."

"Was she seeing anyone?" asked Odelia. "Boyfriend? Girlfriend?"

"She had a boyfriend. Mitch. Mitch Utz," he clarified when Chase started jotting down the name. "She'd been seeing Mitch for a while now." When Chase quirked an inquisitive eyebrow, he said, "Two years now, I think? Something like that. He's a great fella."

"One other thing," said Chase. "One of her neighbors told us she introduced herself as Dotty Berg?"

"Dotty Berg," the man repeated, clearly puzzled. "But her name isn't Berg, it's Ludkin. Dotty Ludkin."

"No idea where the name Berg could have come from? A nickname, perhaps?"

The man slowly shook his head. Clearly this was a surprise to him.

"Okay, we'll leave it at that for now," said Chase, tucking away his notebook and placing a comforting hand on the man's shoulder. "Is there anyone who can be with you, Mr. Ludkin?"

"Yeah," he said, still looking pretty stunned. "Yeah, my girlfriend."

We left Dotty's dad in the car and returned to the apartment building, where several other police vehicles stood parked, and a small army of neighbors had gathered on the sidewalk to speculate about what was going on.

"Poor guy," said Dooley as we entered the place. "He looked pretty shattered."

"Yeah, he did."

"Must be tough to find your daughter like that. How old do you think she was?"

"You heard Abe. Late twenties, probably."

"And she didn't live at home anymore?"

I gave my friend a sideways glance. "What are you driving at, Dooley?"

"No, I was just thinking that she was in her twenties and living alone. Which is probably the ideal situation for any parent, wouldn't you say?"

"Not so ideal when your only daughter goes and gets herself killed," I pointed out.

"No, there is of course that," Dooley admitted. "So maybe there's a point to be made for kids to keep living at home for as long as possible. At least they won't be murdered."

It seemed like a tough choice to make. On the one hand these perpetual guests at the hotel of mom and dad were a nuisance for any pets sharing the premises, on the other hand there is something to be said for keeping your kids safely at home.

Dotty's neighbor who lived directly below her was an elderly lady named Sybil Garlic, dressed in a floral-pattern housecoat that had seen better days. Her gray hair was done up in curlers from which several strands had escaped and she looked a little annoyed at all the fuss. "I already talked to the police," she informed Chase in truculent tones.

"Just a few more details we'd like to iron out," Chase said soothingly. "You told my colleagues that you heard a fight upstairs yesterday?"

"Yeah, a big fight. Shouting and stomping and stuff being dragged around. I thought they were going to keep at it all day, but then it suddenly stopped and I heard footsteps on the stairs and then it all became quiet."

"Did you happen to see who it was that left?"

"No, I didn't," said the woman, folding her arms across her chest and giving us a sour look.

"What time would you say?"

"Two? Three? Something like that. I didn't look at the clock."

"And I'll bet she did," said Dooley.

"Yeah, I think so, too," I said. She looked like the type of person who likes to keep a close eye on everything that goes on in her neighborhood. Maybe even jot down a few notes, like Chase.

"Any idea what they were arguing about?" asked Odelia.

Mrs. Garlic's gaze dropped down to Odelia's impressive belly and I could tell what she was thinking: why aren't you on a couch with your feet up, missy? But instead, she said, "No, I'm afraid I couldn't overhear. Just a lot of screaming and yelling. Though I have a pretty good idea."

"Yes?" said Chase, his pencil immobile over his notebook for a moment.

"There's been plenty of men in and out of the place these last couple of months. Sometimes as much as two or three a day. One of them must have gotten wind of the others and decided to do something about it."

"You're saying that Dotty had more than one boyfriend?" asked Odelia.

"I wouldn't exactly call them boyfriends," said the woman, giving us a keen look. "In fact I never saw the same person twice. Always different men, mostly at night. Late at night," she added with a meaningful slant to her voice.

"So you're saying... what are you saying, exactly?" asked Chase.

"I'm saying that it wouldn't surprise me if Dotty Berg was a prostitute."

CHAPTER 7

"Do you think we should share Sybil's suspicions with Dotty's dad?" asked Chase as we all got back into the elevator.

"Absolutely not," said Odelia, quite sensibly, I thought. "Right now that's all this is: a neighbor's suspicions."

"It would explain a lot," said Chase. "The men coming and going, the fight Mrs. Garlic overheard yesterday, the... peculiar way the apartment is decorated."

"It does look a little like a house of pleasure," Odelia admitted.

"What's a house of pleasure, Max?" asked Dooley. "And what is a prostitute?"

"Um... well..."

Luckily just then the elevator bumped to a stop and we all got out. Saved by the bell!

And we'd just walked out of the building when Chase's phone sang out a cheerful tune. He picked up with a grunted, "Dolores?" listened for a while, frowned, then said just as curtly, "We'll be there in ten," and disconnected. When

Odelia stared at him questioningly, he added, "There's been another murder. Looks like the exact same MO."

"Another one?" asked Odelia.

Chase gave her a worried look. "Why don't I take you home so you can rest?"

"No way," she said, as she started legging it in the direction of the car. "Let's go!"

"This woman," Chase murmured as he hurried to follow so he could open the door for her.

"Chase doesn't seem happy to have Odelia along with us," said Dooley.

"That's because he's worried she'll overexert herself," I said. "But I guess Odelia knows what her limits are better than anyone. If she's feeling tired she'll simply tell us."

At least I hoped she would. Our human can be pretty stubborn, and she's a born sleuth, eager to find out what's going on even more than the rest of us.

Once we were in the car, Odelia turned back to us—or at least turned as best she could, given the circumstances. "When I picked you guys up just now, what was that thing on the couch with you? It looked like a bat or something. Did it fly into the house?"

"It's not a bat," I said. "It's a dog, and it's now Chase's dog."

Odelia stared at me for a few moments, speechless, then repeated, "Chase's dog."

"Yes, Gran has decided to adopt Windex from the shelter," said Dooley, "and give her to Chase, because she doesn't have time to take care of her. It's very kind of her, don't you think?"

Odelia's face took on a set look, and it was obvious that whatever she thought of Gran's gift, the word 'kind' wasn't part of it. "Windex?" she finally managed. "What kind of a name is Windex?"

"It's the name her previous owner gave her," I said. "A woman named Eileen Dobson."

"Yeah, she's an old lady who had to go to a place where they hate pets," Dooley explained, "so she had to get rid of Windex, and now she's very sad, and she thought we all looked scary, especially Max and Brutus, but also Harriet. She thought I was funny, though, so I guess that's a good thing."

"Windex," Odelia repeated as she turned back to face the front. "Great."

"What are you muttering about?" asked Chase.

"Gran has decided to adopt a dog."

"Oh, that's sweet of her."

"And give it to you."

Chase frowned. "What do you mean?"

"Congratulations, Chase. You are now the proud owner of a dog named Windex. A dog, I might add, who looks like a wingless bat and who's scared of our cats."

"Except me!" Dooley cried from the backseat.

"Except Dooley," Odelia dutifully added.

"Windex," Chase repeated, as if trying to get used to the idea.

"She's going back," said Odelia. "Tonight when we arrive home I'm taking Windex straight back to the shelter."

"Oh, no, Odelia!" said Dooley. "She'll be so sad!"

"I don't care! I'm having a baby, I already have four cats—I CAN'T HAVE A DOG!"

"Breathe, babe," said Chase. "Deep breaths, in and out. That's it."

"Odelia sounds a little stressed," Dooley whispered.

"And you wonder why?"

We'd arrived at a nice house in the suburbs, which looked a million miles away from where Dotty Ludkin lived. It was a freestanding house with a picture-postcard front yard and relatively new. Chase parked across the street and we all got out. I could see that Abe had already arrived, and the police activity was picking up in volume and intensity.

When we walked in, a police officer informed us that the person that was found dead was a Calista Burden, aged thirty-seven, who lived at this address with her husband Dave Burden, though of Mr. Burden there was no trace. A UPS man had discovered the body: he'd rung the bell and when no one opened the door had glanced through the window and had seen the owner of the house sprawled out on the couch so he called the police.

Mrs. Burden was indeed in the position indicated, and as we walked in I had a distinct sense of déjà-vu: the position of the body and the way she had been murdered looked much the same as the earlier scene we'd witnessed at Dotty Ludkin's apartment.

Abe looked up when we entered and gave us an unhappy frown. "Two dead bodies in one day. A bit much, wouldn't you say? Even for Hampton Cove."

"I didn't do it, Abe, if that's what you're suggesting," said Chase.

"No, you probably didn't," the coroner admitted reluctantly. "Well, looks like an exact copy of the other scene. Same nylon stocking—in fact it wouldn't surprise me if it wasn't the one missing from the other place—same way the arms were pinned down, presumably by sitting on them with his knees, which would explain the bruising and the lack of defensive wounds. They even look the same," he said, getting up. "Though this victim is perhaps a decade older than the other one."

"Time of death?" asked Chase as he took in the details of the scene.

"Same. Between midnight and two," said Abe.

"Same killer?"

"I'd say so. We'll have the stockings examined, of course, to see if they're a match. And if they are, chances are that the killer killed first one, then took a stocking to kill the other."

"Who was killed first, you think?"

Abe grimaced at this. "Don't quote me, but I'd say the other girl was first."

One of the officers joined us. "Sir, I talked to one of the neighbors and they claim that Calista Burden was a madam."

"A madam?"

"That she ran a brothel, sir. Everyone knew about it. She has an office in town and she ran her business from there but the whole neighborhood knew and she didn't hide it."

Chase shared a quick look with Odelia. It seemed to confirm Mrs. Garlic's view that Dotty Ludkin had been a prostitute.

"Oh, and also, sir, we found no trace of Mrs. Burden's phone. No computer either."

"So the killer strangled Dotty Ludkin with her own stocking, took her phone and laptop, if she had one, then came here and did the same thing with what could very well have been Dotty's boss. Any signs of a break-in?"

"Yes, sir. The backdoor was forced open. Looks like whoever did this came in that way."

"So he broke in here but not in Dotty's apartment," said Odelia.

"Which means it could be someone Dotty knew," said Chase.

"The boyfriend?"

It was a question that couldn't be answered right now. But definitely something to keep in mind.

CHAPTER 8

We decided to pay a visit to Calista Burden's office in town. It was located at the back of a small shopping gallery that had seen better days. Half of the stores had been boarded up and were eagerly awaiting new tenants, and the other half weren't exactly your high-end kind of stores either. Once we'd passed through the gallery, we reached a section where a few offices were located, one of which was the home of Star Calypso, the business Calista owned. When Chase tried the door, it wasn't locked, and so we stepped inside.

The salon where we found ourselves was pleasantly appointed with plenty of subdued lighting and a dark burgundy decor. The sofas were all gold trim and looked expensive. On it, two ladies were seated, looking up with surprise when we entered. A burly male, a very pregnant woman and two cats probably wasn't their usual clientele.

They were both scantily dressed and extensively made up and looked like models.

"Yes?" asked the first one. "Can we help you?"

"Chase Kingsley, Hampton Cove police," Chase grunted, flashing his badge.

Immediately both women were on edge. The police were not their best friend, the sudden change in their demeanor seemed to say.

"Do you work here?" asked Odelia.

Both women decided to remain mum.

"Did Calista Burden work here? Or Dotty... Berg?"

The woman who'd addressed us frowned. "Why are you asking? Has something happened?"

"I'm afraid so," said Odelia, then walked over to the sofa and lowered herself onto it, watched on by the two women, who were clearly wondering what the heck was going on. "Calista Burden was found dead just now. And so was Dotty Berg. Or Dotty Ludkin."

The two ladies exchanged a look of surprise. "Dead? What do you mean?" asked the most talkative one.

"Murdered," Chase clarified. "Presumably by the same person. So if you could please tell us if you knew either Calista or Dotty we would be most grateful."

"Oh, my God," said the woman, and dropped down next to Odelia, visibly shaken.

Turns out they did work for Calista, in her capacity as owner of this massage parlor, as the ladies referred to Star Calypso. The one who'd addressed us had worked for Calista the longest. Her name was Rilla Nyzio and she had also known Dotty well. The other girl, Tosha Hinchliffe, had only started working for Calista recently, and wasn't much help.

"This is just awful," said Rilla. "I've known Dotty since she started working here, maybe a little less than a year ago? She used to work for a caterer but said it was boring work for a measly pay. Here she had the opportunity to make a lot more money in a short amount of time. And she did. She was probably the most popular of all of Calista's girls."

"Do you recall Dotty having trouble with a customer at any point?" asked Odelia.

"No trouble. She was very well-liked."

"Her boyfriend, maybe? Mitch…"

"Utz," Chase supplied.

"I didn't even know she had a boyfriend," Rilla said.

"She mentioned a boyfriend to me," said her friend Tosha. "Said she hadn't told him about what it was she did for a living. She thought he probably wouldn't approve." She shrugged. "My boyfriend doesn't know either. I'm sure he wouldn't like it if he knew."

"Do either of you maybe have a list of clients of the salon?" asked Chase.

Both girls shook their heads. "Only Calista kept a list of the clients," said Rilla. "She kept it on her phone. All the calls came through her and she made the bookings."

"No one else worked with her?" asked Odelia.

Another shake of the head. "She was very discreet," said Rilla. "Usually when a client liked a girl, he stayed with her. Calista didn't like us to swap clients if she could help it."

"I did have one of Dotty's clients once," said Tosha. "Dotty was unavailable and he ended up with me."

"Do you remember a name?" asked Chase, taking out his notebook.

Tosha frowned. "Um… Dewey something? He owns a car dealership. Sells these really fancy Italian cars. He took me there and I could choose my own car for the night. I chose a red Bugatti. I love Bugatti. Wish I could afford one."

"Must be Dewey Toneu," said Odelia. "I attended one of his VIP customer events where he introduced his latest collection of Italian supercars. A very glitzy shindig."

Chase nodded. "Thanks," he told the two girls, then handed them each his card. "If you can think of anything else, don't hesitate to call."

"There is one other thing," said Rilla. "I just thought of it now. Calista's husband Dave was in here a couple of days ago. Him and Calista had a flaming row. They were in the office at the back, but I could hear them all the way here in the salon."

"That's right," said Tosha. "I was also here when that happened. It was so scary."

"It only lasted about half an hour or so, and just when I was worried that Dave might have done something to Calista, and wondered if we should call the cops, he came storming out of her office and disappeared. He looked as if he could have murdered her."

"Calista's office is at the back?" asked Chase.

"Yeah, I'll show you," said Rilla, and led us in that direction.

"We haven't found her phone," Odelia explained. "So maybe she left it here."

"Impossible," said Rilla with a laugh. "That thing was glued to her hand. She took it literally everywhere. It was her office, her connection to her girls, her clients, everything."

"How was she to work for?" asked Odelia.

"Oh, she was just the greatest. She was like a mama bear to us. If a client got a little rowdy she was the first to tell them to back off or else. She didn't care if she lost that client. Well, here we are," she said as she opened the door and led us into Calista's office.

It was cramped, as offices go, and pretty sparsely decorated, and it only took Chase a quick search to determine that there was no computer and no phone there either.

"Not even a notebook or a calendar," he grumbled as he pulled off his plastic gloves.

"I told you," said Rilla. "She kept everything on that phone of hers. She once told me that if she lost it she'd be ruined.

She never let it lie around. Even took it into the bathroom and kept it next to her bed at night."

Chase and Odelia thanked Rilla, and then closed and locked the door to Calista's office and pocketed the key. He explained that a forensic team would drop by to give the office a more thorough search, and also the rest of place, then told Rilla and Tosha to go home. Star Calypso was now closed for business.

CHAPTER 9

When Marsella walked into Toneu Motors on Rutherford Street, she didn't know what she expected to find. Her fiancé in the arms of another woman? Lipstick on his collar? A girl's nylon stocking in the pocket of his blazer? Whatever it was, she decided not to let this Mary-Lynn control her every thought from now on. She was simply going to tell Dewey what Mary-Lynn had told her and see how he'd react. She reckoned herself to be a pretty good judge of character and his response would probably tell her everything she needed to know.

But when she walked in, she found Dewey ill at ease and looking tense. He was pacing the showroom, where gorgeous Italian cars stood blinking appealingly to anyone who passed by. Only there weren't that many people in the place. A few who were browsing and one who was being shown the interior of a Lamborghini by one of Dewey's salespeople.

"Are you all right, darling?" she asked.

"Will you look at that," he grunted, gesturing irritatedly to a couple who were in the parking lot examining a Ferrari Portofino. They were taking pictures of the car, with the wife posing on the hood while the husband snapped a couple of shots. "I should tell them to buzz off," he said. "I need buyers, not lookers."

"Lookers can become buyers, unless you tell them to buzz off," she reminded him gently.

"I'm sorry, darling," he said, pressing a quick peck to her cheek. "It's just been awfully quiet lately. If this keeps up I don't know what I'll do."

"It'll be all right," she said, having heard this particular lament many times before.

"It's that moron Izban," he said, repeating another one of his favorite gripes.

She placed a hand on his chest. "Listen, we need to talk caterers," she said, hoping to distract him from his worries. "We need to make a decision soon, or else we won't be able to feed our guests."

"Just pick one," he said, clearly not in the mood to talk wedding minutiae.

"I don't want to just pick one," she said. "I want us to pick one together."

"Look, the ones we discussed are all excellent. So just pick one. It's fine."

She studied him for a moment. He seemed more tense than usual. "Are you sure it's just the business that's got you worried?"

He turned to her. "Of course it's the business. What else would it be?"

"I don't know. I just…" She thought about the best way to broach the topic, but then realized that this was neither the time or the place to hold such a delicate discussion. "Why don't we go out tonight? We can visit the caterer at the top of our shortlist and then if we like what he's got to offer we can decide on the spot and lock him down."

"Sounds like a great idea," he said, forcing a smile.

He was an attractive man with a full crop of dark hair, now slightly graying at the temples, and still sporting an athletic build in spite of the fact that he was a good fifteen years older than she was. It wasn't hard to imagine his enduring popularity with the ladies, even as he was nearing the end of his fifth decade. And even though she'd decided against the PI idea, she was still determined to have it out with him once and for all.

You couldn't build a marriage based on lies.

And if he did lie, she'd catch him at it.

When she walked out, she saw Odelia Kingsley walk up, along with her husband Chase, the cop. They were accompanied by two cats, a small sort of grayish-beigeish fluffball and one big and orange.

She offered them a smile in passing and wondered if they were in the market for a new car. It never occurred to her they could be there on official police business.

CHAPTER 10

The owner and proprietor of Toneu Motors didn't look like any car salesman I'd ever seen. For one thing he wasn't overly garrulous and avuncular and didn't try to grab our attention the moment we walked in and extoll the virtues of his exclusive and expensive wares. On the contrary, the man seemed very hard to find. Finally his salesman, who was busy convincing an elderly gentleman that a two-hundred-thousand-dollar car was exactly what he needed, steered us in the right direction: the office at the back of the showroom.

Chase knocked on the door and we all filed in without awaiting the man's response. One of the perks of being a cop is that you don't need people's express permission to start bombarding them with all kinds of awkward and sometimes very personal questions. Like whether they enjoy paying for sex on a regular basis.

"Chase Kingsley," Chase curtly announced, flashing his badge. "Dewey Toneu?"

The car dealership owner sat behind his desk, looking

sort of moody and out of sorts. And the sudden arrival on the scene of a cop didn't improve matters much, I could tell.

"Yes?" he said in a sort of surly way, just bordering on incivility. He wasn't going to sell a lot of cars with that attitude, especially at the price points he was advocating.

"We're here to talk to you about your relationship with Dotty Ludkin, or Dotty Berg as she also liked to be called." And to show the other man he meant business, Chase pulled up a chair and plunked himself down in front of Mr. Toneu's desk. Then, when he realized his faux-pas, he immediately got up, and offered that same chair to his highly pregnant wife, who gratefully took a load off her feet and carefully lowered herself onto the chair.

Mr. Toneu stared at Odelia's belly with a touch of alarm, then finally said, "I'm sorry, but there must be some mistake. I don't know any Dotty Ludkin or Dotty Berg."

"And we have it on good authority that you do. To refresh your memory, here is a recent picture of Dotty." He took out his phone and showed the picture Dotty's dad had sent him. It showed the girl in all her youthful splendor. It was taken when she'd spent a day at the beach with her dad.

Dewey stared at the picture for a moment too long, then finally demurred. "Never seen her before in my life."

"Dotty was murdered last night," said Odelia, speaking for the first time. "Strangled to death in her apartment. We talked to one of her colleagues who said she worked for Star Calypso as a call girl. This colleague also told us you were one of Dotty's clients."

"Please don't lie to us, Mr. Toneu," said Chase. "This is a murder inquiry, and frankly I don't have the patience right now to deal with people who refuse to tell us the truth."

Dewey finally relented. "Yeah, all right. I did hire Dotty a couple of times in the past, but this was before I got engaged.

So if you could please not mention any of this to my fiancée?"

"Where were you last night, Mr. Toneu?" asked Chase. "Let's say between midnight and two?"

"Home in bed."

"Can anyone confirm that?"

"No, I live alone. My future wife is conservative that way. She doesn't believe in premarital relations. Wants us to move in together once we're married and not a minute sooner."

"Who is your fiancée if I may ask?"

"Marsella Horowicz. She runs the Vesta Muffin Animal Shelter. I don't know if you know it?" He gave a pointed look at me and Dooley, as if assuming we were well acquainted with the animal shelter. A common misconception, of course. It's not as if all pets like to hang out at night at the shelter for drinks and a pleasant chat.

Chase grimaced. "We know it."

"Is there anything you can tell us about Dotty?" asked Odelia. "Maybe something she mentioned that could shed some light on her murder?"

Dewey frowned. "Like what?"

"I don't know—maybe she felt threatened by a client?"

He slowly shook his head. "Dotty never talked about her other clients. She was very discreet that way. The only person she ever mentioned was some guy who runs a shoe shop, but that's because I'd complimented her on her footwear which I could tell was high quality. She said she got it from Garwen Blemish because he was a regular and he gave her a twenty percent discount. But that was the only time she mentioned a name to me."

"She didn't say anything about being scared or anything?"

"No, nothing like that. She came across as a happy person. Very cheerful. In fact I told her it was a pity she was in the line of business she was in. She was capable of so much more. But she said the money was good, and she liked her boss—more than her old boss at the catering business where she used to work before. Lousy pay and lousy job." He adopted a look of concern. "You're saying she was murdered?"

"Last night," said Chase.

"May I ask how she was murdered?"

"I'm sorry, but at this stage we're not revealing any details."

"I understand." He glanced over to the large window that offered a good view of the showroom. "It certainly puts things in perspective, doesn't it?"

"What do you mean?" asked Odelia.

He produced a sliver of a smile. "Nothing. You won't mention this to Marsella, will you? Like I said, she's very conservative and wouldn't appreciate her future husband hiring an escort, even if it was before we got engaged."

"How long have you been engaged, Mr. Toneu?" asked Odelia.

Dewey picked up a framed picture of what was probably his fiancée and said, "Three months now, though I've known Marsella for years. Took time for her to become convinced of my good intentions but she finally accepted me three months ago."

"So when was the last time you saw Dotty would you say?"

"Must have been last year. Sometime in the fall maybe?"

"And how many times would you say you hired her... services?"

"Not that many. Maybe, like, three or four times, tops."

"And how well did you know Dotty's employer—Calista Burden?"

Dewey shook his head. "I'm sorry, but I don't think I ever met her."

"But you must have talked to her. She was the one who did the bookings."

"It's possible we talked on the phone, but like I said, I never met the woman."

Once we were outside, Odelia said, "He's lying. Ten months ago Dotty was still working for the caterer. She only started with Star Calypso less than ten months ago, and if Toneu was seeing her regularly, there must have an overlap between his time with her and his engagement."

"Can you blame the guy? He doesn't want Marsella to find out he's already been unfaithful to her even though they're not even married yet."

"Poor Marsella. Should we tell her?"

"That she's marrying a possible murderer?"

Odelia stared at her husband. "You think Toneu killed Dotty and Calista?"

"He certainly has a motive: the only way to make sure that Marsella didn't find out about Dotty was to silence both her and her boss."

"So why didn't he silence Tosha? She's the one who gave us Toneu's name."

"You're right. It doesn't make sense. Besides, Rilla said Calista was very discreet, which stands to reason, as discretion is probably paramount in her line of work."

"Apparently Dotty wasn't as discreet as Calista would have liked, if she gave Toneu the name of one of her other clients."

"Max?" said Dooley as we climbed back into Chase's car.

"Mh?" I said, still thinking things through after this recent interview.

"What were the services Dotty and Calista provided? And why doesn't Dewey want his fiancée to find out?"

I swallowed. "Okay, so you know how people like to kiss other people, right?"

"You mean like Chase and Odelia?"

"Exactly like Chase and Odelia. Only some people have a hard time finding someone to, um, well, kiss?"

"Okay," he said, trying to wrap his head around this strange conceit. "Like Wilbur Vickery?"

"Wilbur is a good example," I said, much relieved. Wilbur runs the local General Store and is a lifelong bachelor, though not of his own volition but because he hasn't found the right woman yet—and probably never will, if his seduction technique is anything to go on. "So people like Wilbur can pay someone to kiss with them, see? And Dotty is such a person."

"People paid her to kiss?"

"Exactly. They paid her really good money to kiss with and Dewey was one of those people. Only Dewey is engaged to be married to Marsella Horowicz, who runs the shelter, and she wouldn't like it if her fiancé was kissing other women now would she?"

"No, I guess she wouldn't," said Dooley thoughtfully.

"So that's why he asked us not to tell Marsella. If we did, she would probably call off the wedding since she feels very strongly about things like fidelity and such."

"I see," he said, though I could tell that he really didn't. Then again, I hoped I'd given him enough food for thought to keep him quiet for a while. These were hard questions and frankly I didn't feel entirely qualified to answer them with authority.

"So... does Dewey pay Marsella, too? For kissing her, I mean."

"Not exactly, Dooley," I said.

"So when you marry a person you can kiss them for free, but when you don't, you have to pay? Is that how it works?"

"More or less," I said with a sigh.

CHAPTER 11

A couple had just dropped off a hamster at the shelter and Shelley had had a hard time containing her disapproval. They said they got the hamster for their daughter but the girl had grown bored with the animal and had moved on to wanting a pony now. And so instead of keeping the hamster like any responsible pet parent would, they'd simply decided to unload it on the shelter.

"People like that should be hung, drawn and quartered," she said as she gently stroked the tiny animal on top of its head. "Don't they know they can't treat their pets like that?"

Gavin, who had been busy sweeping the floor in the reception area, leaned on his broom. "Maybe you should have told them. Kick them a conscience for a change?"

"What difference would that make? They'd simply complain to Marsella and Pimkie would still have ended up in a cage."

"Pimkie? Is that what they called it?"

Shelley nodded. She was busy typing on the computer now, updating the website so potential pet parents would know that Pimkie was in search of a new home. And hopefully a warmer and more receptive one this time. It was one of her eternal concerns that the homes they found for their animals would prove to be unsatisfactory. And since animals can't talk, it was hard to know for sure what happened behind those walls.

"I just wish I could work here full-time, you know," she said. "Instead of having to work at that stupid office dealing with stupid cement. Who cares about cement anyway?"

"You won't be in that stupid office always," Gavin reminded her. "One day you'll be the big boss, and you can order your flunkies about. You could even tell them to run the store while you spend all your time in here."

She smiled at his naiveté. "It doesn't work like that, Gavin. It's a hands-on business. You should see my dad. He's in there all the time. He works more hours than anyone."

"Same here," Gavin said gloomily. "Imagine me having to run that shoe store for the rest of my life. Talk about a death sentence."

"I thought you liked shoes?"

"It's shoes, Shelley. They're a basic commodity, as in you need to wear them or your feet will hurt. As far as I'm concerned it's not something you can either like or dislike."

"Looks like we're both unhappy with our lot in life then, aren't we?"

"Worst part is that my dad wants me to take over soon. Says we could open a second store and I could run it. Expand our 'empire' as he calls it."

She smiled. "We should run away together, you know. Me to get away from my cement heritage and you from your dad's shoe empire."

"Now wouldn't that be a thing?" said Gavin, returning her smile. "But where would we go?"

"Anywhere. As long as it's far away from here?"

"And what about the shelter?"

Her smile dimmed as she watched Pimkie's hairy little face twitch and his beady little eyes give her what she imagined was a longing look. A look that said: 'Are you going to take care of me from now on, please nice lady?'

She sighed. "Yeah, we can't leave our precious babes behind. That wouldn't do."

"So shoes for me and cement for you and our precious babes on the side?"

Just then, Marsella walked in and Gavin went back to sweeping the floor and Shelley informed the boss about Pimkie's irresponsible pet parents, repeating her earlier lament.

But it seemed as if Marsella had her own problems to deal with, and hardly paid attention.

&

I must confess I'd completely forgotten about Windex, but of course the moment we walked in the door, there she was, sleeping peacefully on the sofa, and in my favorite spot, no less.

"Is that my new dog?" asked Chase as he stared at the tiny creature.

"She's not your new dog, Chase," said Odelia. "She's going back to the shelter ASAP."

But just then Windex opened her eyes and gave us her trademark sad look. I could tell that Odelia's heart melted, and Chase's heart, which he usually only gives to big dogs, opened up to the concept of having a dog that looks like a bat in the home.

"Aww," said Odelia.

"Ooh," said Chase.

Windex sneezed, a funny little sound, then gazed up at

Chase, who bent over, reached out a large hand, and Windex gave it a tentative lick.

"Aww," said Chase.

"Ooh," said Odelia.

"He's so cute!" said Chase, picking up the tiny doggie, now dwarfed in his arms.

"It's not a he, Chase," said Odelia, but already she looked less like a schoolmarm.

"So is Windex here to stay, Max?" asked Dooley.

"Yeah, looks like she is," I said. I took a sniff at the spot where the dog had lain—my spot—and discovered it now smelled fully like dog and not like myself anymore.

I didn't like it.

Just then, Gran walked in, once more without her billionaire appendage.

"Hey, Vesta," said Chase. "I see you decided to give me a dog?"

"Dog? What dog?" said Gran, then caught sight of Windex and said, "Oh, that's right. I completely forgot about that. Cute little fella, isn't he?"

"It's not a he, Gran," said Odelia. "It's a she. And why did you have to go and get Chase a dog?"

"Babe!" said Chase, cutting a warning look at Windex, now asleep in his arms. "She can hear you."

"Why did you get us a dog!" Odelia loud-whispered. "Don't you think four cats is enough for one household?"

"Two households," Gran corrected her. "And please don't give me that crap. Don't you think I've got enough on my plate already? I've been trying to find a Finnish translator but do you think I found one? No, of course not. And meanwhile Dallas took a room at the hotel just because I couldn't get him to understand he can sleep in my room."

"You want Dallas to sleep in your room?"

"Of course! We're engaged to be married, aren't we?"

"Is he even aware of this so-called engagement?" asked Odelia

Gran folded her arms across her chest and gave her granddaughter a scathing look. "Are you calling me a liar?"

"No, but—"

"For your information, Dallas can't wait to get married."

"How do you know if you can't talk to him?"

"I know, all right? You don't have to teach me about men."

"Where is he now, this billionaire of yours?" asked Chase, gently rocking Windex.

"I left him at the hotel. I suggested I join him for a nap but he just kept smiling and muttering something about muffins. I tell you, it's tough, having to deal with this language barrier."

I saw that Dooley was staring up at Chase, who now seemed thoroughly smitten with Windex. "Is Windex going to stay with us forever, Max?" he asked.

"I'm afraid she is, Dooley," I said, watching on as even Odelia seemed affected by the doggie's peculiar charm. A charm I frankly didn't see, to be absolutely honest.

"So now we're going to have a baby in the house *and* a dog?"

"Yeah, looks that way."

"But Max—it's too much!"

"I know, but what can we do?"

"We could keep Windex and tell Odelia to give the baby to the shelter?"

"Shelters don't take babies," I said. "It's probably against the law."

"Maybe they can make an exception for this baby?"

I gave my friend a pat on the back. "It'll be fine, Dooley. Somehow we'll manage."

Though to be absolutely honest I was starting to feel as if things looked very bleak indeed. Dogs may be man's best friend, but if history has proven anything it's that they're not exactly a cat's best friend. And as Windex opened one eye and turned it on me, a shiver ran down my spine. For in that eye I suddenly thought I saw evil personified.

Could it be that Chase was nursing a viper in his bosom?

CHAPTER 12

Later that night, just as we were getting ready to head out to cat choir, Odelia took me aside. "I want you to take Windex along with you tonight, Max," she said.

I stared at her. "What do you mean?"

"To cat choir. I get the impression she's feeling a little lonely, so I want you to take her under your wing and show her the sights. You know, introduce her to your friends."

"But... Windex is a dog," I said. "And my friends are all cats."

"So? I don't see the problem."

"Cats and dogs, Odelia. They don't mix."

"But I thought you got along so well with Rufus and Fifi from next door?"

"Yes, I do. But—"

"Yes?" She fixed me with a sort of baleful eye. Lately Odelia has been very short on patience. Must be the physical discomfort of having to drag all that excess weight around, I guess. One look at her told me I'd thwart her wishes at my peril. So finally I nodded.

"Okay, all right. We'll take Windex along to cat choir."

"Good. I knew I could count on you to do the right thing." And she patted me sort of absentmindedly on the head, which I didn't appreciate in the slightest but decided not to mention. I was starting to see that maybe Dooley had been right all along. That this baby business meant that Odelia had less time to spend showering her affections on us.

And of course if you think about it, it makes perfect sense: if a human is a vat full of affection, and hitherto that affection only had the single outlet: namely their pets, now with the addition of a baby we'd have to share that same limited resource with the tyke.

Worse, since babies are humans, and cats aren't, chances are that the baby would get the larger portion of that limited supply, with us cats being starved of the precious stuff.

It didn't inspire me with a lot of confidence in a bright future, let me tell you.

*C*at choir is a fun affair, and even as we set out on our journey, the four of us can always feel our moods brighten, our senses heighten and the anticipation making us giddy. Tonight there was none of that. With Windex in tow, I felt a distinct sense of dread.

"So where is this cat choir?" asked Windex, who'd had some very nice chow, courtesy of Marge, some very sweet cuddles, courtesy of Chase, and even a quick medical, courtesy of Tex who, even though he isn't a vet in the strictest sense of the word, had given the tiny doggie a quick once-over and had declared her fit for purpose.

The effect of all this attention was that Windex, a shy and timid creature when we first met, had been injected with a dose of self-confidence which showed in her garrulousness.

"At the park," said Harriet curtly.

"And what do you do?" asked Windex.

"We sing," Harriet snapped.

"Ooh, I like that," said Windex. "Me and my human used to sing all the time."

"Do you miss your human, Windex?" asked Dooley. "Cause I think I would."

Windex considered her response, then said, "You know? At first I thought I'd never get over the fact that I'm never going to see her again? But now that I've found this new home with Chase and Odelia, I'm starting to see that maybe everything will be all right after all."

At this, Harriet grumbled something I couldn't quite catch, though I thought I recognized the word 'parasite.' It certainly didn't sound very complimentary.

"And now with the baby underway," Windex continued, "well, I think it was all meant to be, you know."

"What was meant to be?" I asked.

"Everyone knows that dogs like babies and vice versa. It's the old bond between man and man's best friend. Unlike cats, who can be very catty when a newborn arrives in the home, dogs simply adore babies. They feel protective, you see, and guard them with their lives if need be." She shrugged. "I don't know. It just feels right. For me to be here, I mean."

The four of us shared a look of concern. What was this dog going on about? Did she mean that with the baby arriving Odelia and Chase would chuck us out and install Windex in their home instead? That it was out with the old and in with the new for some reason?

But we didn't have time to consider this extremely disturbing prospect, for we'd arrived at the park, and were immediately accosted by our friends, as is usually the case. Harriet went off to talk to her buddies, Brutus scooted off to shoot the breeze with his, and Dooley and I found ourselves saddled with the task of having to take Windex under our wing, as Odelia had instructed, and introduce her to our fellow cat choir members.

I must say she proved quite a hit. It may be the fact that she looks like a bird, and everyone knows that cats are very fond of birds. Or the fact that her sunny disposition was finally asserting itself, after the distressing time she had spent at the shelter. But she soon proved the life and soul of the party, to the extent that Dooley and I were relegated to the sidelines watching on as Windex became the center of attention and we... didn't.

"I don't know what to think about her, Max," Dooley confessed.

"Me neither," I said. "Is she a psychopath dropped in our home to destroy us? Or a sweet soul who's going to make our lives more enjoyable? The jury is still out, I guess."

"She does seem very different now than she was this morning."

"She was fresh from the shelter, Dooley. She was traumatized."

"So why do I have the feeling that soon she'll be settled in our home and we'll be in that shelter, Max?"

"Odelia would never do that."

"I don't know. Maybe Windex is right? Maybe dogs are better suited for when people have babies than cats? They are man's best friend, after all. And we do have sharp claws."

"I know. But we never use them."

"I overheard Chase talking to Odelia about declawing the other day."

I gulped in shock. "Declawing?"

"Yeah. He was asking her if it was a common practice."

"It's a very painful practice, that's what it is. Bordering on the criminal."

"It just goes to show, doesn't it? That Chase and Odelia are concerned."

"They'd never dump us at the shelter," I repeated, but I realized even as I spoke that my words lacked the true ring of conviction. "Well, they just wouldn't… would they?"

CHAPTER 13

At least the next day Odelia took us along with her and Chase to continue their investigation into the recent murders, so maybe she wasn't thinking of replacing us with Windex just yet. Hard to conduct a murder inquiry from a kennel at the pet shelter.

And then of course there's the fact that Odelia can't talk to dogs, so the new acquisition wouldn't perhaps be as useful to her as we have always been.

Something to consider as I still pondered our future fate.

Chase had made an appointment to talk to Dotty's boyfriend Mitch Utz, who worked in the kitchen of The Bonny Piper, a popular restaurant. When we got there they were just getting started on lunch prep. The young man with carrot-colored hair and a florid complexion was due his first break of the day, and took us outside to have a chat. And as he lit up a cigarette, he listened as Chase explained to him what it was exactly that his girlfriend did for a living.

"My God," Mitch said finally, a deep frown of concern cutting a groove in his youthful brow. "A call girl? Are you sure?"

"You mean you didn't know?" asked Chase.

"No, of course not. I thought she worked for a caterer."

"She quit that job ten months ago," said Odelia. "And started to work for Calista Burden. Though she also called herself Calista Dunne—her professional name."

"Just like Dotty was also known as Dotty Berg," Chase explained.

"I'm sorry, but this is all news to me," said the young man. "She told me about the catering stuff. Even told me stories about her colleagues, about their customers, the jobs she did. Last week she told me about a wedding party they were catering. Her job was the reason she always had to work nights and why we hardly ever saw each other. I'm always here during the day, you see, and she mostly worked evenings, sometimes late at night."

"You never noticed anything out of the ordinary?" asked Odelia. "The fact that she invited men to her apartment?"

"Strikes me as odd you wouldn't have known about that," said Chase. "When even the neighbors knew that the place was always full of strange men coming and going at all hours of the day or night."

But Mitch stubbornly shook his head. "I swear she never told me anything about that."

"So what did you fight about the day before yesterday?" asked Chase, deciding to take a gamble. "One of the neighbors heard you and Dotty. Said it sounded as if furniture was being thrown around."

"That wasn't me, sir," said Mitch earnestly. "Must have been one of those other men."

"When was the last time you saw Dotty?" asked Odelia.

He thought for a moment. "Must have been... a week ago? We were actually going to spend Monday night together."

"The night she was killed?"

Mitch nodded. "Monday is my day off. We were going for

dinner and a movie. But something came up. She had to leave early because one of her colleagues had called in sick. So she ended up bailing on me and I went to see the movie by myself."

"What movie was that?" asked Chase casually.

"*Turtle-Man 4*. The new Marvel movie with Al Pacino and Meryl Streep."

Just then, Mitch's boss stuck his head out the door to see how much longer we were going to keep the kid, and Chase's phone chimed and he reluctantly picked up.

"Do you believe him, Max?" asked Dooley as Chase talked into his phone and Odelia wrapped up the brief interview and offered Mitch her card.

"I'm not sure. He seems sincere enough."

"But how could he not know that she was a call girl?"

"If they hardly saw each other, it could have made it easier for her to lie about her secret life. Her dad didn't know about that side of her either, and he probably saw her more often."

Chase ended the conversation and thoughtfully tapped the phone against his chin.

"Who was it?" asked Odelia.

"Rilla Nyzio. Said she remembered something that she reckons might be important. Calista ran a second business. Wives could hire her to test their husbands and see if they took the bait. If they did, they knew their husbands weren't as faithful as they claimed to be. If they didn't, they could rest easy. She even offered a discount for fiancés. Take them for a test run, so to speak. And get this. Dotty was her number-one girl for this special service."

"You're kidding."

"No, I'm not." He quirked a meaningful eyebrow. "And guess who's getting married soon."

"Dewey Toneu."

"Think that maybe our friend Toneu wasn't as forthcoming as he claimed? That maybe Dotty tried her routine on him and he took the bait and they were going to tell Marsella?"

"If that's true, it's one hell of a motive for murder."

"I'll say it is."

"What are they talking about, Max?" asked Dooley.

"Well... you know how a married couple promise each other to be faithful?"

"Uh-huh."

"Calista was running a business that tested this promise. If Dotty could seduce a husband or a fiancé to, um, kiss her, that meant he'd failed the fidelity test and they informed the partner. If he couldn't be seduced, he passed the test and everything was hunky-dory."

"And now they think that maybe Marsella hired Calista to test her fiancé?"

"It's a distinct possibility," I said. "And if they did, and he failed, maybe he found out about the test and killed them both before they could tell his future wife."

"That reminds me of *Passion Island*, Max."

I laughed. "It does, doesn't it?" *Passion Island* was a reality show Odelia had infiltrated a while back. It involved couples being sectioned on two different islands, the men on one island and the women on the other, with both being subjected to temptation. It was pretty perverse, if you ask me, but then a lot of these so-called reality shows are like that now.

"Do you think a lot of men failed Calista and Dotty's fidelity test, Max?"

"No idea, Dooley. But looks like they found their niche."

"And paid for it with their lives."

CHAPTER 14

Our next port of call wasn't one of my favorite places to be, even though it was named after Dooley's human. The Vesta Muffin Animal Shelter had been founded by Charlene and Uncle Alec in Vesta's honor, though apart from the name she wasn't actively involved. It certainly was a big improvement over the old pound, which didn't hold a lot of fond memories for any of us. At least Marsella did a great job at the new shelter, and treated the animals she housed there with the kind of tender loving care one would hope to see.

"You're here about Windex, aren't you?" said Marsella when we found her in the reception area of the shelter. "So how is she settling in? Fond of her already, are you?"

"Absolutely," said Chase. "She's a lovely little thing. But we're actually not here to talk about Windex, Marsella."

"Oh?"

"I don't know if you've heard," said Odelia, taking over, "but two women were found murdered yesterday."

"Dreadful business, isn't it? And you're in charge of the investigation, Chase?"

"Yes, I am. So we talked to some of the girls who worked for Calista Burden, and they told us she took on clients who paid her to seduce their future husbands."

Marsella stared at the detective, clearly not having expected this. "Come again?"

"One of the two women who was murdered," said Odelia, "Dotty Ludkin, seduced men to see if she could get them to be unfaithful to their wives or future wives. And then Calista would inform their partners about the result of this so-called fidelity test."

"So now we were wondering…" Chase began, but stopped when Marsella held up her hand.

"I know what you're going to say, and the answer is no. No, I didn't hire these people to spy on my fiancé."

"It's not exactly spying," Odelia clarified.

"I know, but I didn't do that. I would never do that."

"You and Dewey Toneu are engaged?"

"Yes, we are, but I didn't hire anyone to try and seduce him. So you can put that theory to rest right now, detective, and look for your culprit elsewhere. It certainly wasn't me."

"We were thinking more of Dewey," Chase admitted. "If he hired Dotty's services—"

"He didn't. Dewey simply isn't that kind of man. He doesn't need to hire anyone's 'services' because very soon he's going to be a happily married man." She spoke these words with some vehemence, as if trying to impress it upon us that we were barking up the wrong tree.

"All right," said Chase. "I believe you."

"You'd better, cause it's the truth." She looked up when she noticed a young blond woman standing at the entrance. How long she'd been standing there was hard to know for sure, but it certainly seemed to annoy Marsella to a certain extent. "Yes, what do you want, Shelley?" she asked with a hint of iron in her voice.

"I've finished cleaning out the cages," said Shelley, giving her boss a look of uncertainty.

"Thanks. You can go now."

"See you tomorrow," said Shelley.

"Yes, see you tomorrow."

The girl dawdled for a moment, then turned on her heel and left.

And so did we, since it was clear from Marsella's demeanor that she had nothing more to tell us.

We caught up with Shelley as the girl mounted her bicycle.

"How much of that did you overhear?" asked Odelia kindly.

The girl's cheeks flamed. "I... a lot, actually."

"How well do you know Marsella?"

"Pretty well. We've always had a great relationship. Which is why I was surprised that she was so snappish with me just now."

"Do you think she might hire an escort service to try and seduce Dewey?" asked Chase.

The girl hesitated, clearly uncomfortable to divulge her boss's secrets.

"It's important," Odelia stressed. "Two women were murdered, and we're trying to catch the person responsible. So anything you can tell us that might help..."

"Of course," said Shelley, nodding. "The thing is that several of Dewey's old girlfriends have contacted Marsella recently, trying to warn her about him. Apparently he has quite a reputation as a ladies' man, and even dated five women at the same time for a while, until they all found out about each other. It's all Marsella can talk about lately, what with the wedding coming up and all. I told her to hire a private detective and have him followed around, just to see if he's still involved with other women, but she said just this morning that she decided against it. She's simply going to trust Dewey. He says this was all years ago and he's a different man now, but I don't know." She gave a light shrug.

"So you think Marsella might have hired Dotty Ludkin to test Dewey?" asked Chase.

"Honestly? I can totally see her do a thing like that. Though if she had, she probably would have told me. We've become very good friends ever since I started volunteering here, and she's been pretty open with me about her doubts and frustrations."

"Okay, thank you, Shelley," said Odelia. "We appreciate your honesty."

"Please don't tell Marsella," said Shelley. "It's a delicate subject."

"We already got that impression," Chase grunted.

CHAPTER 15

Back in the car, Odelia and Chase discussed their most recent interviews. Dooley and I sat quietly in the back, not feeling one little bit at ease, I must say.

The trip to the shelter had brought back the notion that Windex was in our own home right now, sleeping on our couch, eating our food, and generally making herself comfortable in our favorite spots—possibly even relieving herself in our litter boxes!

It wasn't a pleasant prospect, and one that made me positively afraid for the future.

Snippets of conversation drifted in our direction.

"Not a single fingerprint found at either crime scene, can you believe it?" Chase was saying. "Which means the killer wiped everything. Every surface which he possibly could have touched. No phones, no laptops, no trace of any electronic device, so he took them all."

"There must have been something on those phones that could point to him," said Odelia.

"Absolutely. We already talked to the provider and I've

got officers poring over both victims' list of calls but so far nothing that stands out. And listen to this: no calls to connect Calista and Dotty or even any of the other girls."

"They must have kept in touch some other way."

"Probably some secure app that the provider doesn't have access to."

"It doesn't look so bad, does it, Max?" said Dooley, interrupting my musing.

"What doesn't?" I asked.

"Well, the shelter, of course. If Odelia is really going to replace us all with Windex, there are probably worse places to be than at the shelter. Marsella seems like a nice person who really loves her pets, and so does Shelley." He gave me a hopeful look. "Maybe they could adopt us? I wouldn't mind living with Shelley. I think she's a sweet person."

"Odelia isn't going to replace us with Windex, Dooley," I said, though I couldn't conceal the note of disquiet in my voice as I spoke these words. "And we're not going to live at the shelter."

"Shelley is still young," said Dooley. "It's probably going to be years before she gets married and has a baby. So that's great news for us. Or even Marsella. If she gets married she's probably too old to have babies, so that's even better news. Though I don't know about Dewey. He doesn't strike me as a cat person for some reason. So if I had a choice it would be Shelley all the way."

I smiled at my friend. "Shelley it is, then."

"Fingers crossed she's a cat person, Max."

We'd arrived back in town, and Chase parked in front of a shoe store called Blemish & Sons. If the window display was anything to go on, they mainly dealt in expensive shoes.

As we stepped into the store, the little bell by the door jangled merrily. An old-fashioned device, but then the store had apparently been in business for a long time.

A man walked up to us, rubbing his hands with anticipatory glee and immediately darting a glance down to Chase and Odelia's feet. He appeared to be in his late fifties and looked slim and trim with bland features and a neatly combed but thinning mane.

"What can I do for you folks?" he asked. But when Chase flashed his badge, the gleeful hand-rubbing stopped and the smile vanished. No shoes would be sold today, he knew.

"Garwen Blemish?"

The man's head bobbed up and down nervously.

"I hope you can answer a few questions if you don't mind," said Chase.

"Of course," said Garwen, a look of suspicion having crept into his eyes.

"Do you know this person?" asked Chase, and held out his phone.

The man hesitated, glanced up at Chase, saw the implacable look there, and relented. "Dotty," he said finally. "Dotty Berg. Yes, I dated her a couple of times in the recent past. I read about what happened. Terrible news. She was just the sweetest soul imaginable. Though I saw that in the newspaper they referred to her as Dotty Ludkin."

"She called herself Dotty Berg when dealing with clients," said Chase, causing the other man to slightly wince.

"I honestly didn't see myself as a client," he said. "Okay, so I paid her some expense money, but we had such a great time together that it didn't feel like she was a girl for hire."

"Did you drop by her apartment?"

"Oh, sure. Very neat and clean it was. She was very proud of the place. Even though she didn't own it, she was hoping to raise enough money to buy her own place very soon."

Chase gestured to the shoes on display. "You offered her a generous discount?"

"Yes. Yes, I did. We all need shoes, don't we?" he quipped,

then faltered and swallowed. "Look, can you please not mention any of this to anyone? Especially my boy. He doesn't need to know that his old man has to pay for female companionship. And my customers don't need to find out either. It would only serve to damage my reputation and in my line of work a reputation is everything, isn't it? What is it they say? Takes a lifetime to build and seconds to destroy? Well, I can't afford that, to be honest. And neither can Gavin."

"Gavin is your son?"

He nodded. "So can we keep my name out of the papers, please?"

"I don't see why not," said Chase. "Providing you're not involved in what happened."

"Oh, but I'm not, I swear. I mean, I liked Dotty a lot. Like I said, we got along great."

"How did you communicate with her?" asked Odelia.

"They used some kind of app," said Garwen. "She showed me how to install it."

"Dotty?"

"No, the other one. Calista. It's a simple messaging app. She said it's very private."

"Can you show us?" asked Chase.

"Sure thing," said the shoe salesman, and took out his phone. He swiped it to life and showed Chase how the app worked. "See? It's just like Whatsapp and Messenger and Telegram and all those other apps. Only this one can't be hacked. Or so she told me."

"Swiffr," Chase murmured as he studied the man's phone. "I see that you contacted Dotty last month?"

"Yeah. Last time I saw her. She said she was going to be busy and suggested I go with one of her colleagues. Tosha or Sosha or something. I met her once but we didn't click. Not like Dotty. So I told her I'd wait until she was available." He gave them a sheepish look. "I know what you're thinking. Old fool fell in love with a prostitute. But it wasn't like that. You see, a widower like me, of a certain age, doesn't have an easy time finding someone new. I tried dating, but that didn't work. So finally a friend suggested Calista. I talked to her once and based on the interview she set me up with Dotty. And I have to tell you that she was like an angel sent from heaven. Okay, so I paid to be with her, but when you date a person you also pay: dinner, movie, presents... At least with Dotty I didn't have to play games or pretend to be someone I'm not just to make a good impression. She just made everything so easy, you know. No complications." He sighed. "Can't believe she's gone."

"One last question, Mr. Blemish," said Chase. "Where were you two nights ago?"

"Home in bed. And before you ask: yes, I was alone and no one can vouch for me."

Just then, the door of the shop opened and a blond-haired young man entered.

"Well, happy to help, officer," Garwen immediately said, his voice taking on a different, more energetic tone. He pressed Chase's hand. "And I hope you find the hoodlum."

It was a clear indication that the interview was over. And as we walked out, I noticed the similarity between Garwen and the new arrival. No doubt the Son in Blemish & Sons.

*

"What was that all about?" asked Gavin as he watched the highly pregnant woman and the muscular cop get into the police pickup parked across the street. There were also two cats with them, which puzzled him a great deal. Did the police use cats these days?

"Oh, something about a car that was vandalized last night. They wanted to know if I saw anything or if I had a camera pointed at the street. Unfortunately I didn't see anything, did I?"

"Damn vandals," Gavin muttered. "Haven't they got anything better to do than to destroy other people's property?"

"Yeah, tell me about it," said his dad. "So where were you this morning?"

"At the shelter," said Gavin with a shrug.

"Don't you think you're spending way too much time at that place?"

"No, Dad, I don't," said Gavin, not feeling in the mood to take up this discussion again.

"If they really want you to help out all the time, they should pay you. You shouldn't be expected to work for free."

"We talked about this, Dad. They rely on volunteers like me. They haven't got the funds to pay people."

"Sounds like a scam to me," his dad grumbled. "I need you here at the store, Gavin. At least three customers walked back out this morning because I was busy. That's a lot of business we're losing just because you decide to spend all your time over at the shelter."

"So? Hire a salesperson. I don't mind."

"Well, I do mind. Your place is here. It isn't called Blemish & Sons for nothing. Or don't you want to take over the store one day?"

He considered telling his dad exactly what he could do with his store, but since that didn't seem like a good idea, and he didn't want to hurt his old man, he shrugged. "I'm here now, aren't I?"

"All right. You can start by stocking those boxes over there. It's been so busy I haven't had time to put them away."

"Fine," he said. If there was one thing he hated even more than helping indecisive clients try on dozens of shoes, it was cleaning up the mess they left. But since this was apparently his life now, he slouched over to the minor shoebox pyramid and got started.

CHAPTER 16

We were back at the office—Chase's office, that is. One aspect of being a police officer that is often underestimated is the paperwork that comes with the job, and also the number of reports and information that needs to be gone through. The small and dedicated group of officers that assist Chase had produced a small pile of reports that he was now diligently going through one by one. Odelia, meanwhile, took this opportunity to rest in the armchair that was part of Chase's office furniture. She had closed her eyes and was practicing her breathing exercises, trying to relax. Her hands were on her belly and she looked hot and bothered, her cheeks flushed and her brow beaded with moisture.

"Are you all right?" I asked, but she waved my question away with an irritated gesture.

"I guess she is," said Dooley, who had watched the scene with rising concern.

"We should probably give her some space," I whispered to my friend.

"Being pregnant is not a lot of fun," Dooley whispered back.

Chase suddenly whistled through his teeth. "Listen to this," he said. "Dewey Toneu's financial records. His business isn't doing so well. In fact if it weren't for a big financial injection made by Marsella last year, he might even be on the verge of going bust."

"Marsella invested in Dewey's business?"

"To the tune of a hundred thousand dollars."

"So if the wedding should be called off for some reason..."

"Dewey would have to pay back the money. Which I don't think he can."

"Which would be the end of Toneu Motors." Odelia had opened her eyes. "We better have another chat with Dewey. And can we take a look at his phone?"

"You mean check if he's got the app installed?"

"And when he last contacted either Dotty or Calista."

She had closed her eyes again and was fanning herself with a limp hand.

"We can, but if he refuses we're going to need a warrant to confiscate his phone." He gave Odelia a look of concern. "Are you all right, babe?"

"I'm fine," she said, even though she didn't look fine to me. "So can you ask my uncle if he can arrange the warrant?"

"Honestly I don't think we have enough on the guy yet."

"Just ask him. He might disagree. Is it hot in here or is it just me?"

"I'm taking you home," Chase said, getting up. "You need to rest."

"I'm fine, I'm telling you. So what's next?"

Chase sat back down. "Calista's husband is back from his business trip. We can go talk to him now."

"I wonder how much he knew about his wife's business."

"We'll find out soon enough." He directed another anxious look at her. "Are you sure—"

"I'm fine!"

And so she was—maybe.

We soon returned to Calista's house, where this time the door was opened by a swarthy man with gray hair. He didn't look very happy to see us, if the scowl on his face was anything to go by. But when he noticed Odelia's state, he immediately allowed us in and even helped her to a chair and offered her a glass of water.

"I got back as soon as I could," he said, also taking a seat. "I work for Merkel, a big pharmaceutical wholesaler. I'm vice president of sales and had back-to-back meetings all day yesterday and the day before. The moment I got your message I jumped on a plane." He gestured to a pair of suitcases by the door. "In fact I just arrived."

"So you know about what happened to your wife?"

"Yeah, dreadful business," he said, dragging a distraught hand through his wiry mane. "Who would do such a thing? An intruder, you think? Though your colleague told me over the phone that nothing was stolen, so that doesn't seem to make sense."

"We think it might have something to do with Star Calypso," said Chase.

"Did you know what business your wife was in?" asked Odelia.

"Oh, absolutely. Me and Calista kept no secrets from each other."

"Did she... personally get involved with the clients?" asked Chase.

"No, nothing like that. She employed about half a dozen girls but she never dated any of the clients herself."

"What was your opinion of the line of business your wife was in, sir?"

He laughed a curt laugh. "You mean did I mind that she

ran an escort service? No, actually I did not. I'm not a prude, detective. Perhaps there were some questionable aspects about my wife's business, from a moral point of view, but first and foremost it was just that: a business. A buyer and a seller agree on certain terms and conditions and who am I to question their right to do so? As long as nothing untoward happened, or illegal, it was perfectly fine by me. And as far as I know the whole thing was aboveboard."

"One of the girls who worked for Calista told us you and your wife had a fight at the office last week. What was that all about?"

"Just one of those husband-and-wife disputes that are all too common in a long marriage. In fact I don't even remember what exactly started it. Probably the fact that I couldn't make it to a dinner she'd arranged with some friends of ours. We both led busy lives and sometimes things didn't work out."

"Can you tell us where you were two nights ago, Mr. Burden?"

"I told you. I was in Texas for meetings with our sales team. You can ask the hotel. And you can ask my secretary about the meetings. She'll be able to give you all the details."

CHAPTER 17

J was actually starting to get a little peckish, and as luck would have it, Odelia and Chase decided to drop by the same restaurant we'd visited the day before. And if there's one thing I know about restaurants it is that they serve food—even to pets like us.

A police officer had shown a picture of Dotty's boyfriend to the neighbor who'd heard the altercation the day of the murder, and this time she admitted she had indeed seen his face and it was Mitch who left immediately after the fight. So it was safe to say we needed to have another chat, since he'd declared it couldn't possibly have been him that day.

Once more he was called away from his urgent duties in the kitchen, much to his chef's annoyance, to talk to us.

"Okay, so it was me. It must have slipped my mind. You know how it is."

"No, I don't know how it is, Mr. Utz," said Chase. He'd planted a hand against the wall next to Mitch's head and was leaning in. "So please tell me so I do."

"I found a guy's underpants in Dotty's bed and when I asked her about it she confessed that she hadn't worked for that caterer in months and was now working for a dating service, as she called it. Men paid her to go on dates with them and that was it. Which still didn't explain the underpants. So she finally said she worked for Star Calypso, which isn't so much a dating service as an escort service and that she occasionally took her clients home with her. She said she was doing it for us, to save enough money so we could buy a place of our own and move in together. The caterer didn't pay a lot and my job here pays me a pittance, and with the escort stuff, money was rolling in." He shrugged. "So we had this big fight about it. I told her to quit Star Calypso and she said only a couple more months. I didn't like it and I told her so. And she said it was her life and I wasn't the boss of her. Anyway, we didn't part on good terms, which of course I now deeply regret."

"You didn't return that night to have it out with her again?"

"No, I didn't. She texted me but I didn't text back. I was pretty upset when I found out what line of work she was in. And even more upset she didn't bother to tell me about it."

"Did you know Dotty's boss? Calista Burden?"

"No, I didn't. Dotty might have mentioned her, but we never met."

"You could have found out where she lived by trawling through Dotty's phone."

"I didn't. I'm telling you, after we fought I didn't go back there. I was too upset."

"So can you think of anyone else who could have done this to Dotty?"

The guy thought for a moment. "She did mention that a neighbor had started some kind of a campaign against her. Wanted to get her kicked out by the owner."

"What kind of campaign?"

"Putting flyers in tenants' mailboxes warning them of

immoral activities, scratches on her car and dog poop smeared on her windshield. Anonymous letters to the owner. That kind of stuff. She was pretty upset about it. Couldn't wait to get out of that place."

"Did she tell you who she thought was responsible?"

"She didn't know, but she did send me a picture of one of the flyers. Wait, here it is."

"Can you send that to me?" asked Chase, studying the picture in question.

"Sure thing," said Mitch.

What wasn't a sure thing, apparently, was our food. And as Chase and Odelia made to leave, it was against our silent protestations. Frankly we would have protested more vociferously but at this point we were afraid to evoke our humans' displeasure. When they've already got a replacement waiting in the wings, so to speak, it's best you stay out of their hair as much as possible. Let lying dogs lie, and humans, too.

"I'm hungry, Max," said Dooley.

"Me, too," I said miserably.

"Maybe we should tell Odelia to keep a small sampling of kibble in the car, so she can feed us when she's doing these long interview sessions that just seem to go on and on and on. My brain doesn't function when I'm not fully fed."

"Same here," I said. "Good idea about the kibble, by the way. Though I'd hold off on it for now."

He gave me a keen look. "Until we know more about the Windex situation, you mean?"

"Exactly. We don't want to give Odelia an excuse to kick us out."

"So you also think she's going to kick us out?"

"I'm starting to lean toward that point of view," I admitted reluctantly. "Especially after the way she snapped at us at the office."

"She did snap at us, didn't she?"

"She absolutely did. Which isn't like her."

"It's the baby. It's making her cranky." His eyes suddenly widened. "Max! It's the baby!"

"I know it's the baby, Dooley."

"No, but I mean, don't you remember that movie we saw a couple of months ago?"

"What movie? What are you talking about?"

"Satan's spawn, Max! Satan's spawn!"

"Was that the name of the movie?"

"Odelia's baby belongs to the devil! He must have somehow managed to possess her and now she's expecting his baby and it's making her behave very weird. Like adopting a dog, and snapping at us."

I stared at my friend, and resisted the urge to take his temperature.

"Oh, Max, we have to save her. Once this baby is born it's going to be too late!"

ઠ

We were back with Sybil Garlic, and this time Chase was confronting her with a picture of the flyer. The corners of the woman's lips turned down as she took a good look. "Yeah, that might have been me," she admitted. "Can't have a prostitute living in the same building with nice and decent folk like myself. I wasn't having it, and so I decided to do something about it." She stabbed Chase's chest with a bony finger. "You should thank me for doing your job. This is all your fault for taking your eye off the ball, young man."

"How is that?"

"You know the deal. Girls like Dotty and her customers bring in all kinds of problems. Drugs and violence. It's all connected, everybody knows that. Gang lords, sonny. It's all about gang wars and terrible stuff happening to innocent people like me. And think about the property value. This is a good neighborhood. We don't need the likes of her coming here and dragging everything down. Pretty soon this place would have turned into a slum, with drug addicts shooting up in the corridors and littering the place with their needles."

"What else did you do, except this flyer?"

"I may have written to the owner, telling him about the kind of person living in his apartment. He has a right to know."

"And what about the dog poop and the keying of Dotty's car?"

"I don't have a dog," she said, as if this absolved her.

"Of course you don't," said Chase.

Odelia produced a small groan, and Mrs. Garlic directed a look of concern at her. "Are you sure you don't want to sit down, honey? If you don't mind me saying so, you don't look so hot." And to Chase: "If I were you I'd take her straight to a hospital."

"I'm fine," said Odelia, repeating her new mantra. "Absolutely peachy. In fact I've never felt better." And to prove her point she displayed a tired smile.

"Where were you two nights ago between midnight and two o'clock, Mrs. Garlic?" asked Chase.

"What kind of a question is that? I was in bed, of course, minding my own business, just like you should, young man, instead of asking me how I like to spend my nights."

"Are you married, Mrs. Garlic?" asked Chase with a tight smile.

"For your information, I am not. Not that it's any of your business. Now if you're done asking me all kinds of very inappropriate and frankly rude questions, I think I'd like you to leave now." And to show us she meant what she said, she closed the door in our faces.

"Looks like we're done here," Odelia quipped, and it was nice to see her smile again.

"Oh, no, we're not," said Chase, glowering at the closed door. And he was about to apply his fist to the panel when Odelia stayed it in mid-flight.

"It's no use," she said. "She won't give us anything. And besides, there's a big difference between smearing dog poop on someone's windshield and murdering two women in cold blood."

"Yeah, I guess you're right," said Chase, much sobered. "Possibly plummeting property prices probably aren't a good enough motive for a double homicide. And besides, she doesn't look like she's got the strength to strangle two women."

"Oh, I think she's a lot stronger than she looks. But she's also a lot smarter than that. So can we go now? Frankly I've seen as much of this place as I can stomach for one day."

CHAPTER 18

"Okay, so what have you got for me, people?" said Uncle Alec. "And it better be good."

We were in the big man's office, with Chase and Odelia being asked to give the chief of police an overview of the state of the investigation as it stood at that point. Which, to be absolutely honest, was absolutely nowhere. But since no cop worth their salt likes to convey such a gloomy message to their commanding officer, Chase and Odelia launched into an extensive list of potential suspects and their possible motives.

"I think we both like Dewey Toneu for this, don't we, babe?" said Chase, taking a firmer grip on his notebook.

"Toneu as in Toneu Motors? The guy who sells those fancy Italian cars that no one can afford?"

"Yeah, he was one of Dotty Ludkin's clients, and has admitted as much. Though he claims he hadn't seen Dotty since he got engaged to Marsella Horowicz."

"Toneu and Marsella are engaged? That is the first I'm hearing of this." He didn't seem particularly pleased to hear that the woman running the animal shelter was engaged to be married to a possible murderer. "Does Marsella know about his predilection for hired amorous encounters?"

"I don't think so. Toneu was very insistent we don't tell her."

"I'll bet he is," the Chief grunted as he malevolently stabbed his blotter with his pencil.

"Toneu claims he was home alone that night—he and Marsella haven't moved in together yet. She doesn't believe in premarital relations and they'll start cohabiting once the wedding vows have been exchanged and the marriage has been duly registered."

"I see," said the Chief. "Possible motive being that he didn't want his fiancée to find out about his liaison?"

Chase and Odelia both nodded. "Calista Burden—or Dunne as she called herself—had started a sideline," Chase explained, "whereby women hired her to seduce their partners and find out if they were as faithful as they claimed to be. It was Dotty's job to do the seducing. And seeing as she already knew Toneu from before, it's not hard to see how she could have offered her services to Marsella, if the latter wanted to put her fiancé to the test."

"This Calista sounds like an enterprising person," said the Chief admiringly. "She really found an interesting little niche for herself, didn't she? So you think Toneu failed the test and decided to get rid of the evidence by murdering the two women who knew about it?"

"Especially," said Odelia, "since Toneu's business is in trouble and Marsella has made a substantial financial investment in her fiancé's dealership to keep it afloat. If she were to discover that her future hubby has been unfaithful she might call off the wedding and demand he pay back the money, which would mean he'd have to declare bankruptcy."

"Also," said Chase, "we talked to Shelley Eccleston, who volunteers at the shelter, and she says Marsella has had her doubts about the wedding for some time, with several of Toneu's old girlfriends suddenly crawling out of the woodwork to warn her about the guy and claiming he's quite the ladies' man. So I totally see her hiring Calista to take Toneu for a spin—though of course she denies everything and so does he."

"You're right. I like this guy more and more for this," said Odelia's uncle, cheering up. "In fact I like him so much I might be induced to apply for a warrant for his arrest."

"There are other suspects, Chief," said Chase. "There's another client of Dotty's named Garwen Blemish, who runs a shoe store and doesn't want his liaison with the girl to come to light. Figures it will reflect badly on him and might damage his reputation."

"Doesn't sound like a very strong motive," said Uncle Alec. "Alibi?"

"Home alone, just like Toneu. He's a widower," Chase explained.

"And then there's Calista's husband Dave," said Odelia, "who claims he knew about Star Calypso and was okay with it, but who knows? Two witnesses heard him and Calista fight the other day. He says it was a minor spat between husband and wife and doesn't remember what it was about, but according to our witnesses it sounded pretty serious."

"Like you said, maybe he wasn't as okay with his wife's line of work as he says he is," said Uncle Alec, nodding. "So where was he? Also home alone?"

"In Texas at a sales meeting," said Chase. "I checked the hotel and he did check in and spend two nights there, but who's to say he didn't sneak out at some point and fly back here to murder his wife and fly back? Though I admit that does seem very unlikely."

"Did you check possible flights?"

"Still working on that, Chief."

"Okay, go on. Anything else?"

"Well, there's Dotty's boyfriend Mitch Utz," said Odelia. "He also got into a fight with his girlfriend, on the day of the murder, as witnessed by one of Dotty's neighbors. He denied it at first, but when we confronted him with the evidence, he admitted he'd just found out that Dotty wasn't working for a caterer as she claimed but as a call girl. And I think it's safe to say he wasn't happy about it. Not happy at all. He told her to quit and when she said she wouldn't he blew his top."

"So where was he?" He held up a meaty hand. "Don't tell me. Also home alone?"

"No, he went to see a movie. Him and Dotty had arranged to have dinner and see a movie but she ended up bailing on him so he went by himself." And before the Chief could ask, he quickly added, "And yes, I did check, and no, nobody remembers seeing him at the cinema, but of course that doesn't mean he's lying."

"It also doesn't mean he didn't do it," said Odelia. "Since the movie ended at ten and time of death was between midnight and two. Plenty of time to head on over to Dotty's place, kill her and then drive across town to Calista's and take care of her."

The Chief sat forward. "So how did he strike you, this Mitch Utz? Is he capable of murder, you reckon?"

Chase and Odelia shared a look, then both shrugged. "Hard to say," said Chase finally. "He doesn't have any priors. Never been arrested. Not even as much as a parking ticket. By all accounts a decent guy. Comes from a good family. So I really couldn't tell, Chief."

"No, me neither," said Odelia, shaking her head. "He seems like a levelheaded young man. But then of course you never know. Finding out that his girlfriend was a call girl could have made him snap. It has happened before."

"Yeah, I could see him strangle Dotty in a fit of rage, but

then to drive across town and kill Calista?" said Chase. "That's premeditated murder, and that doesn't fit his profile."

"Mh," said the Chief, leaning back again. "Okay, so that's it? Dotty's clients Dewey Toneu and Garwen Blemish, Calista's husband Dave and Dotty's boyfriend Mitch?"

"There's also the neighbor," said Chase. "Sybil Garlic? She was engaged in a one-woman campaign against Dotty, trying to drive her out of the apartment. Put flyers in people's mailboxes, smeared dog poop on Dotty's car, wrote letters to the owner. Basically tried to damage Dotty's reputation and force her to move out. Claimed her presence was driving down property prices and would attract all kinds of unsavory characters."

"Apart from the harassment campaign, she seems harmless enough, though," said Odelia. "A little dotty and spiteful but not really killer material, I'd say."

"Fair enough," said Uncle Alec. "So plenty of suspects, not a lot of alibis and so far nothing conclusive that really points to one person in particular if I understand you correctly."

"That seems to be about the gist of it," Chase admitted.

"Well, then get me something, people. Go find me a smoking gun, for crying out loud."

"You mean a pair of smoking stockings," Odelia quipped, but judging from her uncle's unhappy expression her attempt at levity didn't go down well with the chief of police.

"Just get me results," her uncle growled, tapping the blotter with a pudgy finger. "You wouldn't believe how many phone calls I've received over this. A double homicide in the middle of tourist season? The entire council is up in arms and even Charlene is frantic. Not to mention the head of the chamber of commerce and every storeowner in town."

"We'll find you your killer, sir," said Chase. "And that's a promise."

"Don't think I won't hold you to that, son." Then he

frowned at Odelia's sweaty face and her protruding belly. She'd gone back to her breathing exercises, releasing her breath in little puffs. "And you—shouldn't you be resting instead of gallivanting all over town looking for a killer?"

"But you just said—"

"I know what I said, but I wouldn't be much of an uncle if I didn't put the health and safety of my beloved niece first and foremost, now would I?"

"I'm fine, Uncle Alec," said Odelia with a grimace.

"You don't look fine."

"Well, I am," she said, getting up with some effort. "As long as people stop asking me if I'm fine, I'll be just terrific, thank you very much!" And with these words, she shuffled out and slammed the door.

Uncle Alec turned to his deputy. "She shouldn't be running around in her condition."

"Try telling her that, Chief. She'll bite your head off and stomp on your remains."

"Yeah, I get that impression." He sighed. "Well, don't let me keep you. And please, whatever you do, keep a close eye on Odelia for me, will you, buddy? She's my favorite niece."

"She's your only niece, Alec."

"Exactly."

CHAPTER 19

"We forgot to mention Dotty's dad as a potential suspect," said Odelia once we were all back in the car.

"He's not really a suspect, though, is he?" said Chase, starting up the vehicle with a roar. "At least I don't think he is—do you?"

Odelia thought for a moment, then shook her head. "No, I don't see him murdering his own daughter just because she's in a line of work he didn't like."

"So what do you think, Max?" asked Dooley. "There are a lot of suspects, but who did it?"

"Honestly? I have absolutely no idea," I said. To be fair, my mind had been more focused on this whole Windex business, and so far I'd only been along for the ride as far as the murder inquiry was concerned. Which wasn't a good thing, I know, and I was letting my humans down big time. But when a cat is fighting for survival, frankly all other stuff kind of fades into the background.

And I know we should have talked things through with Odelia, but she looked so out of sorts that I didn't want to bother her with our personal hang-ups. Besides, I had the impression that she was like a powder keg and that she could explode the moment you said the wrong thing. Even Chase was walking on eggshells right now, and he's a burly fella, never afraid to go mano a mano with suspects a lot taller and bigger than him.

"I think Dewey Toneu did it," said Dooley. "He allowed himself to be seduced by Dotty, maybe for old time's sake, and didn't want his fiancée to find out, because it would ruin him. So he killed the two people who knew about his transgression and then got rid of the evidence by taking their phones and laptops and wiping his fingerprints."

I gave my friend an approving look. "Very good, Dooley. Spoken like a true detective."

He glowed with pride, and seemed to grow a few inches, too. "I'm learning from the best," he said modestly. "And from the best I mean you, Max," he hastened to add, in case it wasn't clear.

"I'm not the best by any stretch of the imagination, my friend," I said. "If I were, I'd have figured it out already. As it stands, all I can think about is Windex, and how precarious our position in Odelia's home suddenly seems to have become."

He nodded sagely. "It's a troublesome state of affairs," he declared. "Very worrying."

I stared at him. "You're pretty relaxed about it, though. Why is that?" Usually when something of this magnitude happens, Dooley is all atwitter, a knot of panicky nerves and a bundle of anxiety. Now he seemed pretty laid-back, which was out of character for him.

"Sometimes you simply have to accept the unacceptable, Max," he said, sounding like a wise old man all of a sudden. "So I'm learning to accept my fate. Odelia is going to give birth to Satan's baby, who will take over their lives, along with Windex, and we're going to be adopted by Shelley or Marsella, though I'd much rather prefer Shelley, of course, since I don't like Marsella's future husband. Though if he's the killer, he'll probably be out of the picture soon, and then Marsella will be all alone and won't mind taking in four cats."

"I hate to break it to you, Dooley," I said, "but it would be a rare thing for any person to adopt four cats at once. One, maybe two at the most."

My words had an alarming effect on my friend. His jaw dropped and his face morphed into a mask of shock. "But Max, they can't pull us apart! That's non-negotiable!"

"I'm afraid that's the way it is. Just like when siblings are adopted the adoptive parents usually take one and then a different set of adoptive parents take the brother or sister. It's not pleasant but that's the way it is." I gave him a sad look. "At least Marsella and Shelley appear to be friends, so chances are that we'll still be able to see each other from time to time." But then I slapped my brow. "Duh. Of course we'll still see each other. We'll meet at cat choir, won't we? You and me and Harriet and Brutus? Unless of course Shelley is one of those people who lives in an apartment and doesn't allow her cats to go outside. In which case we might never see each other again for as long as we live."

"Max, but that's horrible! That's terrible! That's the end!"

I shrugged. "Just the way the cookie crumbles, I guess."

"But we have to stop them! I can't imagine being cooped up in an apartment and never seeing you again—or Brutus or Harriet or even Kingman or Buster or Shanille or, or, or..." He gave me a look of utter and total dismay. "This is just the worst—the absolute worst."

"I know," I said with a sigh, and lay down on the backseat, prey to a sudden dark gloom.

Dooley was quiet for a moment, then he seemed to steel himself. "I know what we should do."

"What?"

"They can't solve this murder without you, can they? I mean, for as long I can remember, you've solved all of their cases for them. In fact there's not a single case they've solved on their own, without your help. So why would this time be different?"

"I don't know if that's necessarily true," I said. "If it weren't for them, I'd never be able to cobble this stuff together." As cats we don't have the luxury to go around flashing our badges and knocking down doors and interviewing people. For one thing cats don't have pockets to put those badges, and for another we don't have the sturdy boots to knock down doors. Also, people feel awkward answering questions directed at them by what they obviously consider to be an inferior species. And then of course there's the fact that they don't understand a word we say. All hurdles Chase or Odelia don't necessarily face.

And it's worked out well for us so far. They ask the questions and collect the evidence, and I sort through it and tag along like the interested observer that I am and at the end of the day, if things work out, I try and come up with the answer. And of course they get all the credit, since I'm not precious in that way. Not a bad deal, as deals go, I should say.

"Well, I say it's true," said Dooley. "Name me one single case they've managed to solve all on their own, without any help from you?"

"Well, um..." I thought for a moment. "Charlie Dieber's bodyguard?"

"You caught his killer."

"Um... Randy Hancock?"

"All you."

"What about Chickie Hay, Lil Thug and Dick Dickerson?"

"You, you and you. No, it's no use," he said when I opened my mouth to speak. "Without you none of these vicious killers would have been brought to justice. So I'm going to say it now, Max, and please don't argue with me: you are indispensable. And so here's what we're going to do: if Odelia and Chase decide to put us all in the shelter, you tell them there will be no more assistance from you in solving their cases. None. And no more valuable tips from us for Odelia's articles. The well is going to run dry. We're going on a strike, Max. A sleuthing strike."

I stared at my friend. Had he really come up with such a luminous idea all by himself?

"So what do you think, Max? Are you with me or not?"

For a moment, I couldn't speak. It was the sheer emotion preventing me from giving utterance to my extreme gratitude.

Dooley must have misinterpreted my silence, for he said, "You think it's a lousy idea, don't you? I should have known. I'm not an ideas cat, Max. I may be a loyal sidekick, but the bright ideas are always you. Just like Dr. Watson never had all that much to contribute, or that goofy Captain Hastings. I'm sorry for even mentioning it, but I just thought—"

"It's brilliant, Dooley," I finally managed in a husky voice. "Absolutely brilliant."

His face lit up like a Christmas tree. "You think so?"

"Of course!" Then I sagged a little. "Though I'm not sure if it will make any difference. You seem to overestimate my role in this household, buddy. I may have a great idea from time to time, but at the end of the day it's Odelia and Chase who carry out the investigation. And it's they who set the trap and make the arrest. Not me."

"And I think you underestimate the important part you play, Max," he said warmly.

I smiled at my friend. "At least you've managed to lift my mood—even if only for the briefest of moments."

Besides, who was to say that Windex wouldn't prove ten

times the sleuth I was? In which case she'd be the one riding with Odelia and Chase from now on. She'd be the one pouncing on clues and sorting the red herrings from the true gems.

Then again, as things stood, it was still us in the car, and not that tiny batlike dog, and so for what no doubt would be our last hurrah, I decided to pay attention once more to the investigation, discover who the killer was, and then tell Odelia that she was only getting a name from me if she promised—preferably in writing and with her signature confirmed by two reliable witnesses in front of a notary—never to take us to the shelter.

It might work, or it might not, but it was the only shot we got, as Bruce would say.

CHAPTER 20

We were back at the Toneu car dealership, where Dewey Toneu seemed very unhappy to see us again. When Chase steered his car into a parking space in front of the shop, I could read Dewey's lips as he turned to his colleague and cried, "Not them again!"

And as we waltzed into the showroom, Dewey had that set look on his face that told me he was gearing up for a fight. He came walking up to us with an energetic gait, ready to rumble, but Chase stopped him dead in his tracks when he waved a document in the man's face. "Your financial records, Toneu. Why didn't you tell us you're virtually broke?"

The man immediately turned back to this same employee, who stood standby in case things got ugly and his boss gave the sign to muscle these annoying cops out of the showroom, and said, "It's all right, Pedro. Go and see if Suzy needs help at reception."

Pedro gave Chase the dark look of a loyal servitor, nodded once, and stalked off.

"Why didn't you tell us this before?" asked Odelia, though she probably should be used to it by now that people very rarely told the police the truth. It seemed a tough habit to break.

"Look, it's not what you think," said Dewey.

"Your fiancée invested a hundred thousand dollars in your company, Mr. Toneu," said Chase, relentlessly pursuing his line of inquiry. "So if she discovered that you were seeing Dotty, I think it's safe to say she would have canceled the wedding, and demanded that money back."

"Which gives you one heck of a motive for murder," Odelia concluded.

"Yes, I know how it looks, but I didn't kill Dotty, all right!"

"You're not denying that Toneu Motors is in serious financial trouble?" asked Chase.

"No, I'm not denying that. But you have to understand that circumstances haven't exactly been ideal. We were doing fine until Peter left."

Chase arched a quizzical eyebrow, the way he did so well.

"Peter Izban," said Dewey. "He used to work here as one of my salespeople. Top salesman of the year three years in a row, in fact. Until he decided to go into business for himself and set up shop across the street and take half of my customers along with him." He gestured through the floor-to-ceiling glass that constituted the front of his showroom at another car dealership, inconveniently located right in front of us. The sign said 'Izban Motors' and the kind of cars that littered the lot appeared to be much the same ones that Dewey sold. "He nearly ruined me when he left. And if that wasn't enough, he's been bad-mouthing me with the customers that chose to stay. Telling them I overcharge, that I deliver shoddy work etcetera etcetera. That bastard is costing me some serious money."

"Can't you sue him for stealing your customers?" asked Odelia.

Dewey grimaced. "They left here of their own free will, didn't they? Nothing I can do about that."

"Defamation of character? Slander?"

"Oh, he's very clever, Peter is. He'll never come right out and tell people I'm a crook, but the way he says it sure sounds like I am one." He rubbed his hands. "And yes, Marsella has been so kind to invest money in my business, and yes, if she were to decide that the wedding is off I'd probably be ruined. But I'm telling you, I hadn't seen Dotty in months. I truly love Marsella, and the last thing I want is to screw up my one shot at happiness."

"Marsella has been receiving messages from your old girlfriends," said Chase. "Telling her to watch out and explaining to her what kind of man she's getting involved with."

He ground his teeth as a dark look came into his eyes. "I know. She told me."

"Tell us again where you were the night Dotty and Calista were killed?"

"How many times!" the man said, his anger flaring. But looking into Chase's cool blue eyes he quickly simmered down. "Like I told you before, I was at home. Alone."

"You didn't take your car for a spin? Have a little drive?"

"No, I arrived home around eight, prepared dinner and ate it in front of the television."

"What did you watch?"

"A game. Cowboys against the Giants."

"Pretty dumb move from Hernandez in the first quarter, huh?" said Chase, studying the man intently.

"It's not the first time he fumbled a pass," said Dewey, relaxing a little and puffing out his chest. "I mean, Jackson was wide open, for crying out loud!"

"Yes, he was," said Chase, and darted a glance over to that same loyal retainer, presumably one of Dewey's salesmen, who stood eyeing us from a distance, no doubt wondering why the police had dropped by again and if he should tackle Chase in case he decided to make an arrest. "All right, Mr. Toneu," he said, pressing the other man's hand. "Please don't leave town."

"But I have a convention I need to be at in two days," said Dewey, his face sagging.

"Then I'm afraid you'll have to send someone else."

"But—"

"Two women were murdered, Mr. Toneu," said Chase, towering over the man. "You were involved with one or both of them. You don't have an alibi. And you had good reason to get rid of them. So I'd say that makes you the perfect suspect in my book."

"Okay, all right," said Dewey, holding up his hands in a gesture of defense. And as we walked out, he called out after us, "Any time you want to take her for a spin, just let me know, Mr. Kingsley—Mrs. Kingsley!" And gave us an exaggerated smile and wave.

"So what do you think, Max?" said Odelia, once we were outside and Chase was checking out a nice secondhand Alfa Romeo.

"I have no idea," I told her—and I wasn't lying.

She frowned at me. "You must have some idea."

"Max isn't going to help you anymore, Odelia," said Dooley.

"What are you talking about?" she said, not all that friendly.

"Unless you put it in writing that you won't dump us at the shelter."

"God, I really don't have the time or the energy for this nonsense," she muttered, and joined Chase, who was letting his hand glide across the car's upholstery for some reason.

Dooley and I exchanged worried glances.

"It's true, Max," Dooley finally whispered. "She's going to get rid of us!"

"Yeah, it certainly looks that way," I agreed, also whispering my words.

"Maybe we should run away, Max. At least that way we'll always be together."

"I don't know. Maybe we should wait and see? Odelia hasn't really been herself lately."

"It's like I told you, Max—she's pregnant with Satan's spawn! Just like in the movie!"

I'd finally remembered the name of the movie. "You mean *Rosemary's Baby?*"

"Let's just call this what it is… *Odelia's Baby!*"

I shivered. It had been a particularly scary picture, and we'd all spent half the time underneath the couch, and the other half hoping the movie would be over soon. The only one who hadn't been bothered was Gran, who had found the whole thing extremely funny for some reason. But then Gran usually laughs when she should be scared, and gets upset when a movie is supposed to be funny. I guess she's not as attuned to Hollywood's output as the rest of us. Or maybe she's just wired differently.

"Max, they're leaving us behind already!" Dooley suddenly yelled.

I looked up and saw that Chase and Odelia were indeed crossing the road.

We quickly got a move on and hurried after them.

"See? She was going to dump us at the car dealership!" Dooley said.

"Well, she's not getting rid of us that easily," I returned, vowing to stick to our humans like a poultice from now on.

CHAPTER 21

When we arrived on the other side of a fairly busy road, we saw Chase and Odelia enter the Izban Motor dealership, presumably to have a chat with Peter Izban. We arrived just in time to slip through the door, and sat, panting heavily, counting our lucky stars that we'd made it without a scratch on our persons, though it had been a close call.

Peter Izban was a string bean of a fellow of about thirty, with nicely coiffed hair and a face that reminded me of a ferret. I wouldn't have selected him as salesman of the year even once, but then perhaps he had other assets that trumped his unfortunate outward appearance. And indeed, once he started talking, I knew what these assets were: he had a deep, sonorous voice that inspired confidence and the urge to take out your wallet.

"I think I have exactly what you've been looking for," he said, darting a quick look at Odelia's belly. "Nice family car of excellent design and with a solid five-star safety rating."

"We're not here about a car," said Chase curtly.

"Oh? But I saw you across the street, visiting my friend Dewey Toneu?"

"Which is what we wanted to talk to you about," said Chase, flashing his badge.

There was a slight lessening of the man's warmth, but to give him credit, at least he didn't get mad, like Dewey had done. "So what can I do for you, Detective Kingsley?"

"You used to work for Dewey, is that correct?"

"Oh, absolutely. Worked there for years. Wonderful boss, Dewey, absolutely wonderful. I learned so, so much from that man. He was my mentor in every possible way."

"And still you decided to quit and strike out on your own?"

He smiled, and a bucktooth became evident. It didn't detract from his charm, though. It might even have added to it. One of those perfect imperfections you hear so much about. "You know how it is. At the end of the day we all want to be in business for ourselves. No offense to Dewey, but he did run a pretty tight ship, and I've always dreamed of being my own boss one day. So when the opportunity arose, I decided just to go for it, you know. With Dewey's full blessing, I might add. That's the kind of guy he is."

"Is it true that you took half of Dewey's customers when you... went for it?"

He laughed a sort of careless laugh that didn't entirely ring true. "Is that what Dewey told you? I'm afraid the truth is more prosaic. I'd built up a close relationship with my customers and once they heard I was setting up my own shop they decided to give me the benefit of the doubt and take my new place for a spin." He shrugged. "And they must have liked what they got, cause they decided to stick with me ever since. And who am I to tell them they should have stayed with Dewey? I'm simply glad they paid me the greatest compliment a customer can pay any business: by placing their trust in me."

"So you haven't been spreading rumors about Dewey being a lousy mechanic, overcharging his clients and being on the verge of bankruptcy, now have you?"

"Oh, absolutely not," said Mr. Izban virtuously. "I would never do such a thing." But then he gave us a grin of such dishonesty it was quite obvious that Dewey hadn't lied.

Chase walked up to the man until he was almost nose to nose with him. Peter Izban, credit to him, stood his ground. More or less.

"If I hear one more word about your unsavory business practices, Izban, I'm going to come down on you like a ton of bricks. I'm going to turn this place inside out, going over every receipt with a magnifying glass, every tax return, every bank statement, every sale. I'm going to talk to your staff, your suppliers, and every single one of your customers and when I'm done I'm going to do it all over again. Until I find something that isn't up to snuff and when that happens I'm going to tear you limb from limb. Do you understand?"

The man gulped, his eyes bulging. "Y-y-yes, detective," he said in a squeaky voice.

"Make no mistake, I believe in free enterprise. What I don't believe in are crooks who believe they can run roughshod over another man and destroy his business so they can get ahead. Frankly I find that kind of behavior repulsive."

"No, absolutely."

"Now tell me, do you recognize either of these two women?" asked Chase, and showed the man pictures of Dotty and Calista.

Izban shook his head vehemently. "Never seen them before, I swear."

Chase studied him for a moment, then finally relented. "Don't forget what I told you."

"No. No, of course not."

When we finally walked out of the place, I saw Peter Izban insert a finger between his neck and his collar and pull, hard. I had the impression he'd had quite the epiphany.

This time at least when we crossed the road, Chase was so kind to pick us both up and carry us, even as he helped his wife across by staring down every driver who thought crosswalks are a quaint notion to be taken as a suggestion not a strict obligation.

And he'd just helped Odelia in the car and assisted her in clicking her seatbelt into place when his phone chimed. He took it out and read the message. "Looks like we need to pay another visit to Sybil Garlic," he finally grunted. "She's been posting some pretty nasty stuff on her blog."

"Mrs. Garlic has a blog?" asked Odelia as she closed her eyes for a moment, allowing her head to rest against the headrest.

"It would appear so, and the things she writes about Dotty and Calista aren't very nice to say the least." He tucked his phone away again. "What is it with people? How hard is it to be civil for a change? And what is it about 'love thy neighbor' they don't understand?"

"Let's just go, Chase," said Odelia, who clearly wasn't in the mood for a philosophical discussion about the nature of mankind. "And yes," she added when her husband opened his mouth to speak, "I'm absolutely fine!"

"She doesn't look fine to me," Dooley whispered.

"No, she certainly does not," I whispered back.

"She forgot about us back there, Max."

"I know."

"We could have died crossing that road."

"I know."

"The old Odelia would never forget about us."

"I know, right?"

"What are you two whispering about?" Odelia grumbled without turning.

"Nothing," I said.

"Absolutely nothing at all," said Dooley.

"Good," Odelia murmured. "Nothing is just about all I can take right now."

CHAPTER 22

Once more we found ourselves in the presence of Dotty's slightly less than delightful neighbor Sybil Garlic. And once again she declined to invite us into her little home, opting to engage us in conversation on her doorstep. It made me wonder what she might be hiding in there.

"'Good riddance,' Mrs. Garlic?" asked Chase, reading from his phone. "'Filthy scum got exactly what they deserved?' Is that a way to talk about your neighbors?"

"Okay, so I'm not unhappy that she's dead," said Mrs. Garlic, giving us a pointed look, as if she didn't approve of cats in her home any more than she did ladies of the night. "But that doesn't mean I killed her, now does it?"

"Please try to apply restraint in the things you write online, Mrs. Garlic," said Chase. "Dotty Ludkin had a family. A father who loved his daughter very much. And a boyfriend who felt the same. Do you really want them to read the kind of stuff you write?" When she didn't reply, he said, more forceful this time, "Delete it would be my strong advice."

"And if I don't?"

"I'd be forced to look a little closer into the vandalism charges that have come to light. And trust me, I'd be inclined to take those very seriously indeed."

"You shouldn't be looking at me, you know. I'm not the bad guy here," she said annoyedly. "You should be looking at those men that were up there all the time. She probably thought no one noticed, but I did. Place was like a darn bus stop."

"Was there someone up there with Dotty the night she died?" asked Odelia, getting a sudden moment of inspiration.

"Oh, absolutely. Like I said, there were men up there all the time. It never ended. And then laughing and talking and playing their music way too loud. Her bedroom is right over my bedroom, so I could hear her mattress squeak when she was doing her business. I always had to sleep with earplugs or I wouldn't have gotten any sleep at all."

"You didn't happen to take a look at the person who was up there that night, did you?"

We all stared hopefully at the old lady who wiped her hands on her housecoat. "No, I'm afraid I didn't. Not that night. I usually liked to take a peek through the peephole, just to know what kind of people were entering the building. But not that night. You see, there was a special episode of *Hoarders* on that I did not want to miss. I heard them arrive, though. Her laughing, him talking. So I knew she had company again."

"What time was this?" asked Chase, taking out his notepad.

"Must have been... eleven? Something like that? You could check the TV guide. The show had just started, which is why I remember it so distinctly, cause I even raised the volume on my TV, hoping they'd get the message. Which of course they never did," she added with a touch of bitterness.

"What else did you hear?"

"Well, nothing much. Like I said, I'd raised the volume to drown out her noise." She thought for a moment, leaning against the doorframe. "I did hear him leave again, though. I'd turned off the TV and was getting ready to go to bed so it must have been after twelve. And this time he was alone, so she stayed up there. But then that was her usual routine, or so I understood. She picked up these men in a bar or whatever, then took them back here and after they were done they left. It was no different that night. Only..." She frowned. "I could have sworn I heard someone go up again about ten minutes later. But quiet like. As if they didn't want to disturb anyone."

"Couldn't it have been a different apartment?"

"Not a chance. Next to Dotty lives Mrs. Gardner, and she's out like a light at nine, and hardly ever gets any visitors. No, it must have been Dotty they wanted." She let out a sound of regret. "Now I feel so ridiculous for not taking a look-see." She eyed Chase excitedly. "Do you think it was the killer?"

"Possibly," Chase allowed.

"Damn," said the woman. "Now I could kick myself."

Judging from the look on Chase's face, he wholeheartedly agreed, and might even have agreed to be on hand to do the honors himself.

We'd just made it down in the narrow elevator —another claustrophobic experience—and to the car when Odelia let out a loud cry and sort of collapsed in pain.

"Babe!" Chase said and immediately was there to offer his arm.

She looked up into his face, grimacing painfully. "I think…"

"I know. You're fine, right? Absolutely fine."

She shook her head. "Not this time."

"What do you mean?" he said, and I thought I detected a note of panic in his voice, which to be honest I'd never heard there before.

"Does your offer still stand?"

"What offer?"

"To take me to the hospital? *Ouch!*"

"Oh, dear Lord," said Chase, and immediately tucked his wife into the backseat, then ran around the front of the car, hopped into the driver's seat and slammed the door.

"Hey!" I yelled. "What about us!"

"Chase!" I could hear Odelia shout. "The cats—don't forget about the cats!"

Chase leaned over, shoved open the passenger door and Dooley and I obligingly hopped in. And not a minute too soon, for moments later Chase was roaring away, his blue police light flashing, his siren wailing, and basically racing through town at an unhealthy speed.

"Please try not to crash the car before we arrive," said Odelia.

"Breathe, babe," said Chase. "In and out, in and out." And to make sure his message came across, he proceeded to demonstrate by breathing laboriously and loudly.

Odelia did the same, and because that kind of behavior seems to be oddly contagious, both Dooley and I also breathed in and out, soon falling into sync with our humans.

And so it was that four heavy breathers raced across town, with Chase weaving in and out of traffic and generally making great haste.

Soon we arrived at the hospital and he jerked the car to a stop so fast Dooley and I both ended up in the footwell. Not that I minded. After all, time was of the essence, with Odelia doing a lot of cursing in between all that heavy breathing, and from to time hollering that this was all Chase's fault and she was going to get him for this if she lived to tell the tale!

It was all disconcerting in the extreme, I have to say, and even as Chase went in search of someone who could be of assistance, Odelia said, "I swear to God, I'm going to kill him."

"Who?" I asked, fully bewildered.

"Who do you think!" she screamed, then went into what could only be described as some kind of painful spasm, for her face became contorted and she screamed a long list of profanities I never even knew she knew.

Dooley gave me a look of shock, and I would have covered his ears if I hadn't been utterly shocked myself. Our sweet human had suddenly morphed into a monster!

"Satan's spawn, Max," Dooley whispered. "It's taking her over!"

I didn't know about that, but judging from her red, sweaty, swollen features, something was definitely the matter with her.

But then a nurse came with a wheelchair, and transferred her into it and rolled her away. So we decided to hop out, lest we were locked in there for however long it would take Odelia to deliver this baby. We followed the nurse into the hospital, but suddenly found our progress barred.

"No pets allowed!" someone yelled, picked us up and would have deposited us back outside if Odelia hadn't yelled from her uncomfortable position, "Those cats are mine and they're coming with me!"

"But..." the person said.

"They're coming with me!" Odelia insisted, and gave the person such a fierce look, they immediately set us down again and we toddled in our human's wake.

And so it was that we found ourselves on the precipice of this most auspicious occasion: about to welcome a new person into our family.

CHAPTER 23

Unfortunately we met one final hurdle, and this one refused to budge: even though we made it all the way to the maternity ward, to allow us in the delivery room was never going to happen. And frankly I didn't mind one bit. In preparation for the birth Odelia and Chase had watched a documentary the other day and it all looked very unappealing to me.

So we were relegated to the waiting room, and were soon joined by the others: Marge and Tex were the first to arrive, then Uncle Alec and Charlene made their appearance, and finally Gran and Scarlett showed up, Harriet, Brutus and Gran's Finnish billionaire in tow, who seemed to enjoy the process tremendously, though he did have a sort of puzzled look on his face.

Chase was there to inform the family of the progress, before making his way back to the delivery room like an intrepid reporter returning to the frontline.

Once I thought I heard Odelia scream something about an epidural, whatever that might be, but apart from that the Pooles seemed to settle in for the long haul, with Tex disappearing from time to time only to return with plastic cups of coffee and some sandwiches from the hospital canteen, and Gran's billionaire to disappear, period.

"Where is Dallas?" suddenly Gran asked, becoming aware of a distinct dearth of Finnish billionaires in the room. "Did anyone see Dallas?"

"I loved *Dallas*," Uncle Alec admitted. "Especially when they shot JR."

"Not that Dallas, you fool!" Gran cried. "My Dallas!"

"I think I saw him heading in the direction of the geriatrics ward," said Tex.

"So you still don't speak Finnish, do you?" asked Charlene.

"No, and I have a feeling I never will," said Gran. "It's a tough language to learn. Though I have picked up a couple of words here and there."

"And his English is still nonexistent?"

She shrugged. "I don't know what it is. You'd expect a billionaire to speak the most popular business language on the planet, but apparently not. He keeps repeating my name a lot, so he must be really smitten, but when I think he's going to kiss me, he always has some excuse. Frankly it's infuriating."

"I hope she's all right in there," said Marge, chewing her lip nervously. Obviously she couldn't care less about Gran's billionaire or the language barrier preventing love's young dream from coming to fruition. "Where is Chase? He should have given us an update already."

"She's fine, honey," said Tex, patting his wife's knee and studying a rather large baloney sandwich. He seemed about the only one there who was enjoying himself.

"Why don't you go and have a look?" Marge suggested. "You're a doctor."

"Best to leave them be," said Tex. "We don't want to get in the way, now do we?"

Judging from Marge's expression getting in the way was the only thing she did want.

"So have they got a name for the baby yet?" asked Scarlett. She was dressed in her usual attire: tight shirt, short skirt and plenty of garish makeup.

"I have absolutely no idea," said Marge, pulling a face. "They haven't mentioned anything to you?" she asked her mother.

"Not a thing," said Gran, looking under a plastic chair in hopes of finding her elusive billionaire.

"So is it a boy or a girl?" was Scarlett's next question.

"No idea," said Marge reluctantly.

"I don't think they know themselves," said Gran. "Some couples don't want to know, you know."

"I'm sure they know," said Tex. "Only they're keeping it to themselves."

Marge stared at her hubby in dismay. "You think they know but haven't told us? But why?"

"Honey, it's fine. We'll know soon enough, won't we?"

Marge resumed her position of rigid unease. "The least you could have done was ask Chase. I thought you and he were so close?"

"We are close, which is why I decided not to pry."

"Where is Windex?" suddenly Dooley asked.

"Yeah, where is that weird creature Chase adopted?" asked Gran.

"She wasn't home when we arrived," said Harriet.

"I thought she was with you," said Marge, directing an accusatory look at me.

"No, we left her at the house when we set out this morning," I said.

"God, now we've gone and lost Windex!" Marge cried,

throwing up her hands. She turned to her husband. "Better go and find her, Tex."

"Find who?" asked Tex, having just taken a savory bite from his sandwich.

"Windex!"

"Who's Windex?"

"Oh, Tex," Marge sighed.

"Windex is the dog Chase adopted," Gran explained.

"But I thought you had adopted her?" asked Charlene.

"Me! Why would I want to adopt a dog? No, this is all Chase."

She seemed to have conveniently forgotten that it was actually she who picked Windex up at the shelter, before dumping her in Chase's lap. Then again, she already had her billionaire to think about, of course. One lapdog probably was enough.

"I'm not leaving my daughter to give birth all by herself," said Tex. "Just to go and find some stupid dog."

"Hey, I'll have you know that Windex is a very clever dog," said Gran. "Not to mention part of this family now."

"Don't you think four pets is enough already?" said Uncle Alec. "Why add a dog?"

"It's a nice mix," said Gran after giving this some thought. "These days it's all about diversity, Alec."

"Fine," said Uncle Alec, not wanting to get into an argument with his mother. "Take a dog. Take two or three or four. But with a newborn in the house, it doesn't seem wise."

"Oh," said Gran. Clearly she hadn't thought about things from that angle. But then she dismissed the thought. "Windex is a sweetie. She wouldn't hurt a fly, let alone a baby."

"Still," Uncle Alec grumbled as he stared at his coffee as if it had personally insulted him. "This stuff is even worse than the bilge they serve at the station, if that's possible."

"Have you caught that killer yet?" asked Scarlett, abruptly changing the topic.

"No, we have not," said Uncle Alec, glowering at her.

"With Odelia and Chase here, maybe you should assign the case to a different detective?" Marge suggested.

"There is no different detective. There's only me and Chase."

"So the case is going to remain unsolved?" asked Charlene. "That won't do, Alec."

"They've got it as good as wrapped up," the Chief blustered. "Just a few minor details."

"Like identifying the actual killer," I said, but of course nobody was listening.

"Why didn't you tell us you were working on a case?" asked Brutus. "We could have helped."

"We did tell you," I said. "But you didn't seem particularly interested."

"I'm sure that if you told us we would have remembered," said Harriet.

"Odelia is going to kick us all out and drop us off at the shelter," Dooley announced, dropping his bombshell. "And since pet parents rarely adopt more than one pet, we'll all be split up, and since most people live in apartments, we won't even be allowed to get out and so we won't be able to go to cat choir anymore and we'll never see each other again."

Harriet and Brutus gawked at Dooley and both struggled to find speech. Harriet was the first to put into words her extreme displeasure. "But they can't! They just can't!"

"I already suggested we go on a sleuth strike," Dooley continued, "but when we told Odelia she didn't seem impressed."

"To be fair, she did have other things on her mind at the time," I said. Like having a baby.

"But I don't want us to be split up!" said Harriet, tears of righteous fury in her eyes. "If this is true, I'm running away. And you have to run away with me, starfish. We'll live on the streets, feed ourselves from dumpsters. It won't be fun but at least we'll be together."

"Of course, starshine," said Brutus, though the notion of having to feed on dumpsters seemed to put a damper on his excitement for his true love's escape plan.

"If Clarice can do it," said Harriet, referring to a feral friend of ours, "we can."

"Absolutely," said Brutus with a distinct lack of enthusiasm.

"What are you guys going on about?" asked Gran. "What's all this nonsense of you living out of dumpsters when you've got a perfectly fine home? Don't we feed you enough? Is that it?"

"It won't be our home much longer, though, will it?" I said.

"Yeah, Odelia is going to take us to the shelter and leave us there," said Dooley.

"Where we'll be adopted by single-pet parents who'll split us up," said Harriet.

"And then we'll have to feed on rats," said Brutus morosely. "And mice and... rats."

"What a load of nonsense," said Gran. "Where did you get this crazy idea from?"

"Well, Windex is there now, isn't she?" I said. "And everyone knows that people consider dogs much better pets for families with babies. They're man's best friend."

"It's our claws," Dooley said. "In fact I heard Chase ask Odelia about declawing."

"Declawing!" Gran cried, causing the others to all regard her with alarm.

"What's going on?" asked Scarlett.

"The cats think Odelia and Chase want to chuck them

out," said Gran, "because their claws might be dangerous to the baby, and to replace them with Windex."

"Nonsense," said Marge firmly. "Besides, it's not up to Odelia or Chase to decide. And if they do want to keep the cats away from the baby you can all move in with us for a while."

"With me, you mean," said Gran.

"Or they could move in with me," Scarlett suggested.

"Or with me," Charlene said with a shrug. "I happen to like cats."

To say we were all moved to tears by this outpouring of hospitality would be an understatement. Hugs followed, and even Dooley appeared appeased by this denouement. The only one who seemed unaffected was Tex, who was reading something on his phone. "What did you say the name of this dog is, Vesta?" he asked suddenly.

"Windex. Why?"

"Says here that Windex's owner has been looking for him."

"Her," Gran corrected her son-in-law. "What do you mean, looking for her?"

"Just what it says in the paper. 'The daughter of Mrs. Eileen Dobson, who was recently admitted to Cherryvale Nursing Home, has launched an appeal to find her mother's beloved dog Windex. The day Mrs. Dobson was admitted, Windex was accidentally left behind in the apartment they shared. By the time Mrs. Dobson's daughter returned to fetch the dog, she was gone. Mrs. Dobson misses Windex very much, and has offered a reward for her safe return.'" He looked up. "I thought you said you got her from the shelter?"

"I did. They said her owner had gone to a nursing home where pets aren't allowed, so she had to get rid of her."

"Looks like you were fed some wrong information, Vesta," said Charlene.

"Oh, hell and damnation," said Gran. "And now the dog has vanished!"

Just then, Chase appeared in the door. He was positively beaming. "It's a girl!" he cried.

As one person, the whole family rose to their feet to crowd around the young father. "Can we see her?" asked Marge.

"Not yet. I'll let you know when you can," he assured us.

Tex cleared his throat. "So what's the name of my granddaughter?"

Chase gave him a sheepish look. "We haven't decided yet, Dad. Though we were thinking about calling her Ida."

Tex's face clouded. Ida was the name of his least favorite patient.

"Just kidding, Dad!" said Chase, clapping the other man on the back, almost causing him to take a tumble. "And now if you'll excuse me, I'm going to see if I can hold my daughter!"

CHAPTER 24

It took a while, but finally we were all invited to partake in the happy occasion. Chase lifted us all up in turn to take a look, and what we saw was Odelia, looking tired but happy, with a tiny human in her arms. In fact the human looked so small it took me a moment to identify it as human at all. It was wrinkly, red, tiny and generally pretty ugly.

Of course I didn't voice this sentiment, but when finally we had all taken our turn, and were back on the floor, Harriet whispered, "I didn't know that babies were so ugly."

"I know," I said. "And why is it so small?"

"And why are its eyes closed?" asked Dooley.

"And why is so red and scaly?" Brutus grumbled.

Generally it didn't look like anything to be afraid of, though. Not like the formidable enemy Dooley had made it out to be. Satan's spawn it most certainly was not, unless Satan deliberately makes its spawn look as vulnerable and fragile as possible, which is unlikely.

"It does have something, though, doesn't it?" I said finally. "That *je ne sais quoi?*"

"I don't know about that, but it does look sort of cute," said Harriet.

"And Odelia looks very happy," said Dooley. "So maybe we'll be all right."

"Of course we'll be all right," said Brutus. "Didn't you hear what Marge said?"

All in all, I have to say I felt more relaxed and happy than I had in days. And judging from the soft words spoken by the humans in the room, they were all pretty happy, too. So if this is what it was like when a new human arrived into this world, I was beginning to see why they all enjoyed the prospect so much. It truly was a source of joy. Ugly, but joyful.

Odelia was going to stay at the hospital for a few days, and so was the baby. Chase would stay put while the rest of us all got to go home, and tomorrow was another day.

When we arrived home, the Pooles remembered their mission to organize a search for Windex, and so we were all recruited to assist in the search.

"Max and Dooley, you take that side," said Harriet, adopting the persona of fearless leader, "and Brutus and I will go that way. We have to find her, you guys. We have to bring her home!"

"Yes, sir!" Dooley said, and would have saluted if he'd known how.

Harriet took off with Brutus to scour the landscape for a sign of Eileen Dobson's precious little doggie, and so did Dooley and me.

And as we traipsed along the sidewalk in the direction indicated, my friend had a confession to make. "I'm sorry about all that Satan's spawn business, Max. Looks like I overreacted."

"And I'm sorry about the shelter business," I returned. "I also overreacted."

We shared a smile. "So looks like we'll be fine after all."

"Yeah, looks like it," I agreed. "Now all we have to do is find Windex and await Odelia's return with the baby."

"Do you really think they'll call her Ida?"

"Somehow I doubt it."

"They could call her Harriet. Nice name, Harriet."

"We already have a Harriet in the family, Dooley."

"So we could call her Harriet 2. And then when they have another baby we'll call her Harriet 3. And so on. Or we could even call them H2 and H3. That way it's easier for Odelia." He suddenly tooted in my ear, "Dinner is ready, H2 and H3! See? Convenient."

"I wonder where Windex could have gone off to," I said, looking behind a hedge.

"Maybe she went looking for her human?"

"If that were true, she would be there right now, and Mrs. Dobson's daughter wouldn't have launched that appeal."

"Or maybe she returned to the shelter, hoping to find her human there?"

"Possible," I admitted. "But unlikely. I mean, she seemed happy enough to be with us last night. Even excited about cat choir and everything."

"Yeah, the life and soul of the party."

"Harriet and Brutus shouldn't have left her all by herself."

"*We* shouldn't have left her all by herself," Dooley said.

Too true, of course. And we'd just doubled back, thinking maybe to take a look behind the house instead, when I thought I heard Windex's voice. I pricked up my ears, and sure enough it was her. The sound seemed to be coming from the Trappers, Tex and Marge's next-door neighbors. And after we'd wended our way in that direction, we came upon a comforting sight: there she was, Windex, freely shooting the breeze with the Trappers' sheepdog Rufus and Odelia's neighbor's Yorkie Fifi. The three dogs were lying on the lawn in Ted and Marcie's backyard, and obviously having a good time.

"Oh, hey, you guys," said Windex. "You never told me you've got such great neighbors."

"And you never told us," said Rufus, "that Odelia adopted such a great new friend?"

"Yeah, about that," I said, deciding to break the news to the tiny doggie before she heard it from someone else, "your human has been looking for you, Windex. In fact her daughter launched an appeal for you to be found and reunited with Mrs. Dobson."

"But... I thought she couldn't keep me?" said Windex, visibly surprised by this news.

"There seems to have been some kind of misunderstanding," I said. "I don't know how it happened, but when Mrs. Dobson was taken to the nursing home, you got left behind in the confusion of the move. And when her daughter returned for you, you were gone."

"So... she wants me to live with her? At the nursing home?" asked the doggie, perking up at the prospect.

"Yeah, absolutely," I said. "In fact they've been looking all over. Though why they didn't simply contact the shelter I don't know. Then again, maybe they thought you'd run away."

"You are loved, Windex," said Dooley emphatically.

Windex gave him a strange look. "Oh-kay. And so are you, Dooley."

"Thanks," said Dooley, lying down next to the others, satisfied that his work was done.

"So you're leaving again?" asked Rufus. "So soon?"

"But we only just met," said Fifi.

"It's all right, you guys," said Windex. "It's a nursing home, not a prison. I'll be able to sneak out at night, I'm sure. And then I can join you for this dog choir you mentioned."

"We'd love to have you," said Rufus. "We're short on sopranos at the moment."

And so it was arranged. Windex would join dog choir, which sounded like a better proposition for her than cat choir, and before long we returned home, where we bumped into Marge, who had already been in touch with Eileen Dobson's daughter, who was dropping by later to pick up Windex. And true to her word, she did, and we all got to say goodbye to Windex while the younger Mrs. Dobson chatted with Marge and Tex.

Turns out that a neighbor had found Windex on the windowsill outside Mrs. Dobson's house the day of the big move, and had misunderstood something Eileen had mentioned to her earlier, about the home not being amenable to pets. What Eileen had forgotten to mention was that they did make exceptions for small pets like Windex. And so the neighbor, who must have been a little confused, had decided to take Windex to the shelter herself, figuring Eileen had forgotten about her faithful canine companion.

"I had a great time," said Windex, wiping away a tear. "You took me in when I was at a low ebb and gave me a home just when I needed one and I can't thank you enough."

"We could have been nicer," I told her.

"Yeah, we kinda felt threatened by you," Harriet admitted.

"Threatened! But why?"

"We thought you were going to replace us," Dooley said, offering an apologetic smile.

"I would never want to replace you guys," said Windex earnestly.

"I thought Odelia took you because dogs are better for babies than cats," said Brutus.

"Oh, you guys!" said Windex, laughing. "That's crazy!"

"I know," I said ruefully. "And we see that now, Windex."

"It's fine, Max," said the doggie, placing a tiny paw on my

shoulder. "You took me in, you introduced me to a bunch of new friends, and generally I feel like I owe you one."

"You really don't," Harriet assured her. "If anything, we owe you. For your friendship. And for showing us the error of our ways. We were too quick to judge. I was too quick to judge."

"All of us were too quick to judge," I grunted.

"Well, I never noticed a thing," said Windex with a smile. "You were never anything less than nice to me, and I feel like I've made four friends for life these past couple of days. And hey, this is not goodbye. I'll be seeing you around."

"Absolutely," I said warmly.

Several hugs later, we waved goodbye to Windex, and kept on waving until the car turned left at the end of the street and she was gone.

"I miss her already," said Dooley, wiping away a tear.

"We behaved abominably, you guys," said Harriet.

"Yeah, we should have been much nicer," Brutus agreed.

"It's fine," I said. "We learned a valuable lesson."

"That, we did," said Harriet.

"What's the lesson?" asked Dooley, curious.

"That dogs that look like bats aren't necessarily evil," I said. "And that babies that look like wrinkled raisins aren't necessarily Satan's spawn."

"In other words," said Brutus, "first impressions can be deceiving." And as we returned to the house, he said conversationally, "Wanna know what I thought when we first met, Max?"

"Not necessarily."

"I thought you were arrogant."

"Is that a fact?"

"Yep. The most arrogant cat I'd ever met."

"Huh. Odd, that."

"Why?"

"Because that's exactly what I thought of you."

"Ha! You're funny, Max."

"I like to think so."

"So very funny," he said, and clapped me on the back so hard I almost buckled.

Sometimes first impressions can be deceiving. Other times? Not so much.

CHAPTER 25

I wouldn't have minded spending a prolonged time at the hospital, keeping our human company, but hospitals don't seem to be equipped to deal with the presence of pets on the premises. For one thing they don't have a big stock of litter tucked away in the basement, or even bags of kibble for this particular occasion. So it was decided by the powers that be that we'd simply stay home instead. And so that first night it was just us and Chase, and frankly it wasn't too bad. He more or less completely ignored us, and also he forgot to clean out our litter boxes. Plus he forgot to fill up our bowls, but luckily there was still Marge, who took care of all of that and more: she gave us those all-important cuddles.

"So when is Odelia coming home?" I asked the next morning. "Will she have to stay at the hospital long?"

"No, just a couple of days," said Marge as she offered me a bowl filled with yummy wet food that tasted moreish. "If the baby is fine and so is she, she'll be home soon."

"I hope so," I said, then realized how my words might be interpreted, and quickly added, "I mean, Chase is a wonderful pet parent, of course, but we're so used to Odelia—"

"He forgot to feed you again, didn't he?"

Both Dooley and I nodded sheepishly.

"I'll tell him," said Marge, and gave us both an extra-large helping of the good stuff, just to make up for her son-in-law's failings in that department.

"I wonder how he's going to manage with the baby," said Dooley. "Is he going to forget to feed her, too? Or change her diaper?"

Marge grimaced. "Lucky for the little one there's always Odelia, and also there's us."

"Is it true that babies drink milk that comes out of the mother?" asked Dooley. "Like pandas?"

Marge smiled. "Yes, Dooley. Human babies drink milk from their mothers, just like pandas. And in fact all mammals secrete milk for their young ones. It's a common trait."

"Oh," said Dooley, wondering about this strange conceit. "So what role does Chase have to play?"

"I'd say the baby daddy has plenty of important tasks to fulfill in the young one's life," said Marge vaguely, though I had the impression her faith in Chase had taken a hit.

"At the very least he'll make sure that Odelia and the baby are taken care of," I said, coming to Chase's defense. He might not be the perfect pet parent, but he was a good person.

Harriet and Brutus came wandering in through the pet flap and eyed our rather generous helping of food with an eager eye. "Don't tell me, you two haven't been fed either?" asked Marge.

They both shook their heads.

"Oh, dear," said Marge, and took out two more bowls and one more can of food.

I think it was actually Gran's week to provide us with

sustenance, but the old lady had been so busy trying to engage her billionaire in a romantic interlude she'd totally forgotten about us, just like Chase had.

Just then, the man of the hour wandered into the kitchen, gave us all a scrutinizing look and said, "So Odelia told me to take the cats along with me today." It was clear he wasn't entirely sure how to go about this. Then again, cops don't usually take their wives' cats along on their investigations, so I guess he could be excused for his lack of excitement.

"Who wants to tag along with Chase today, you guys?" asked Marge.

"Not me," said Brutus, who had his mouth full of food. "I'm busy."

"I'm also busy," said Harriet, giving her boyfriend a cheeky wink.

I would have asked what they were busy with but had a feeling I probably shouldn't.

"I'll go," I said.

"Me too!" said Dooley.

"So you've got two brave volunteers to ride with you today, Chase," said Marge.

"There won't be a lot of riding going on, I'm afraid," the cop growled. "I need to go over the reports that came in so it's all going to be office work today." He sighed. "In fact I'm not sure there's much the cats can do. They'll probably be very bored."

"Oh no, we won't," I assured him.

"We love office work, don't we, Max?" said Dooley.

"Absolutely. We live for office work," I said.

"Then office work it is," said Marge cheerfully, dashing Chase's hopes that he could walk into his precinct without two cats in tow, causing him to become the topic of a lot of good-natured ribbing.

Marge prepared us what she called a packed lunch and off we went.

"So what are you going to call the baby, Chase?" asked Dooley once we were in the car.

"Better buckle up," Chase grunted. Then he frowned. "Or not. Actually I don't think there's a rule about pets and seat belts, or is there? I'd have to check the traffic code."

"When is Odelia coming home?" asked Dooley. "And where is the baby going to sleep?"

"He can't understand us, Dooley," I said, settling in on the backseat and getting ready for a lazy day at the office.

Marge had told us to take our bathroom breaks outside, since there was a patch of green behind the precinct that was supposedly the backyard but no one had bothered to take care of it so it was more like a wasteland now. And she'd told Chase to make sure to leave the window open when we gave him any indication that we needed to go.

We arrived at the police station and walked in, single file, with Chase taking the lead and Dooley and me right behind.

Dolores, whose domain is the precinct vestibule, had to laugh when she saw us arrive. "Will you look at that," she said. "Papa duck and his two ducklings!"

"Very funny, Dolores," Chase grunted.

"When the Chief told us you'd finally become a father I forgot to ask if they were human. I guess I've got my answer now."

"Ha ha ha. So funny."

She held up her phone to snap a picture of us, and Dooley and I gladly posed. Chase, though, looked about as happy as a man getting ready for a root canal or a colonoscopy.

"Smile for the camera, Detective Kingsley," said Dolores. "This one is going on the station bulletin board."

"Oh, hell," Chase muttered.

"Well, congratulations, buddy," said Dolores, tucking

away her phone. "Everything all right with mother and child?"

"Yeah, they're both doing great," said Chase, leaning on the counter and rubbing his eyes. He yawned. "I was up half the night. And then there's these cats yowling like nobody's business. No idea what they wanted from me."

"Did you feed them? Clean out their litter box?"

Chase stared at her, bleary-eyed. "Litter box?" he asked. "They've got an entire backyard to do their business in, and if that's not enough, they've got those fields behind the house. And as far as food is concerned, there's plenty of mice infesting the place."

"But we don't eat mice, Chase," said Dooley. "We're not *murderers*, you know."

Dolores glanced at us and gave us a look of commiseration. "I've got a feeling these two will be more than happy when Odelia finally comes home again."

"Finally? She's only been gone one night."

"One very long night," I murmured.

When we arrived in the precinct, Chase's colleagues all jumped up to congratulate him, and some of them had even bought gifts. There were nappies—small ones for the baby and big ones for the daddy—though I had a feeling those were just for fun—and of course there was cake and other refreshments and one of his colleagues had even gotten him a complete set of baby clothes. They were very small and very pink.

"So what's the baby's name?" asked one of his colleagues.

"We haven't decided yet," said Chase, giving her a tired smile.

"Call her Vesta, after her great-grandma," said another colleague.

"Anything but that," said Chase with a grin.

"Or Alexa, after her great-uncle!" said another.

"Yeah, right," said Chase. "That'll be the day."

We finally settled in at the big man's office, Dooley and I in a corner and Chase behind his desk, and for the rest of the day we watched him work. He was reading emails, checking phone records, poring over witness statements, crime scene reports, financial records, forensic reports... From time to time he grabbed his phone to talk to one of the people he'd already interviewed, or to consult with Odelia, who gave advice from her hospital bed, and he even took the time to talk to us—though more in lieu of talking to himself.

"Okay, so here's the thing," he said, addressing me as he tapped his pencil against his teeth. "They found Dotty's car nearby, parked on the next block. Only she hadn't used it to drive home that night, since it had collected a parking ticket the night before, then another parking ticket on the night. So she must have arrived home with her killer."

"Sounds like a logical conclusion," I told him.

"Unfortunately there's no CCTV anywhere on her block, or her building. So we have no idea when she arrived home, apart from Sybil Garlic's witness statement, and we have no idea where she was or who she was with. Calista must have known, but she's not around anymore to tell us, so that's a dead end. And if Dotty received instructions about who to meet and where, it was done through the encrypted app Calista used, and since we don't have their phones there's no way to read out that data—even if we could decrypt it. And the company that owns Swiffr is in China, so it's safe to say that's another dead end."

"Have you checked the movements of the different suspects in the case?" I asked.

"We've checked the alibis for everyone Dotty was involved with, and so far we've got nothing," he said, more to himself than to me, for obvious reasons. I didn't mind, though. At least we got an update on the case, even if we couldn't directly participate.

"He's clever, isn't he, Max?" said Dooley admiringly. "And so thorough."

"Yeah, he's a good detective," I said. "Doesn't miss a trick."

Finally Chase threw down his pencil and stretched. "What do you say we visit Odelia?" he suggested.

"Oh, can we!" Dooley cried.

He grinned at our visibly excited response and got up from behind his desk. "I'm not getting anywhere with this, so let's just get out of here, fellas."

And so once more we tripped behind Papa Duck, like the good ducklings that we were, and soon were on our way back to the hospital to visit Mama Duck and the real duckling.

Odelia was doing fine, and so was the little one, but it was obvious she couldn't wait to go home and rest in her familiar surroundings. Even though maternity wards are designed to be hospitable, it's not the same as being in your own home, of course.

"One more night, the doctors said." She glanced down at the little one in her arms. "Though if it were up to me I'd be going home right now." She glanced down at me and Dooley. "And how are you getting on with my fur babies?"

"Oh, they're fine," said Chase. "Spent the whole morning cooped up in the office with me." He took a seat at the edge of the bed. "I have to say their presence is kinda… soothing."

"Isn't it?" said Odelia with a smile.

"Though to be honest with you, this investigation is going nowhere fast."

"You'll get there in the end," she assured her hubby.

Chase wasn't as confident as his wife, but her endorsement bucked him up. "So have you thought about a name yet?" he asked.

She smiled. "I liked that last name we discussed."

"You sure?"

She studied her baby's sleepy face. "Yeah, I'm sure."

"Okay, then I guess it's decided. Welcome to the family—"

"Let's not announce it just yet," said Odelia quickly.

Chase looked down at us. "No, you're right. The walls have ears."

Dooley and I shared a look of concern. I'd never been referred to before as a wall with ears. Then again, maybe she was right. If she told us the name, we'd tell Marge or Gran, and before long, the whole town would know. Clearly they wanted to announce the name themselves, and to the gathered family all at once.

And as the little one slept, and Chase and Odelia watched on with loving pride, Dooley and I curled up at the foot of the bed, and were soon fast asleep ourselves.

It had been a pretty stressful couple of days, and we could use the repose.

CHAPTER 26

Chase had gone home, and so Dooley and I decided to pay a visit to Kingman. The investigation was clearly stuck, and now that Odelia was in the hospital and her focus was elsewhere, there was no sign that things would get unstuck any time soon. It was a little disconcerting, of course, to have two women murdered in cold blood and no killer coming into the frame of the team tasked with his or her apprehension.

"Hiya, fellas," said Kingman, who was lying in front of his human's store as usual. "What's new?"

"Nothing much," I said.

"Odelia's had a baby," said Dooley. "And she's already got a name but we're not supposed to know, because walls have ears. Did you know that walls could have ears, Kingman? Cause I looked very hard and I couldn't find them."

"It's just something people say, Dooley," said Kingman with a light chuckle. "Walls don't actually have ears, unless there's people behind them listening in."

"I think Odelia was referring to us," I said. "She clearly

doesn't want anyone to know the name before they're good and ready to announce it."

"Did they set up a dedicated Instagram page for the kid?" asked Kingman. "Cause that's what a lot of parents do these days."

"Why would a baby need an Instagram page?" I asked. "Aren't they too young to post stuff?"

"It's not the baby that's going to post stuff, silly," said Kingman. "It's the proud parents who want to post pictures of their newborn so friends and family can follow their progress."

"Oh, right," I said. Frankly my mind hadn't really been on the baby all that much. It irked me that we couldn't solve the case, which was definitely a first for me.

"So what's going to happen with you?" asked Kingman.

Dooley and I stared at our voluminous friend. "What do you mean?" I asked.

"Now that the baby has arrived. You'll probably have to move out, right?"

"And why would you think that?" I asked, a fresh wave of concern rippling through me.

"It's obvious, isn't it? Baby comes, pets have to move out. Seems like a natural thing."

"Well, for your information, Kingman," I said, not hiding my annoyance, "it is not."

"No, we're staying put," said Dooley. "Marge promised, and Marge's word is her bond."

"Mh," said Kingman, not hiding his skepticism. "Let's just wait and see, shall we? Wilbur's niece had a cat, a very pretty Burmese, I might add, who got the boot when she had the baby. Cat ended up living with relatives until the baby was big enough."

"Oh, no," I said. "Not this story again!" Frankly I'd had it with fearmongering.

"They promised, Max!" said Dooley, turning to me. "They solemnly swore!"

"And they'll keep that promise, Dooley," I said. "And don't you believe otherwise."

"I won't," he said, but it was obvious that doubt once again held him in its iron grip.

Just then, a woman came toddling up along the street. She was walking with a dog on a leash, and when we looked closer, we saw that it was none other than... Windex!

The woman entered Wilbur's shop, but before doing so tied Windex's leash to a metal bar outside that Wilbur has installed especially for his canine-loving clientele.

"Hey, you," I said, greeting the tiny doggie like an old friend, which she now was.

"Hey, Max. Hey, Dooley," said Windex, looking more happy than ever. "Kingman."

"Windex," said Kingman. "So how are things at the nursing home?"

"Oh, so you heard about that, did you? Well, pretty great so far. They're all treating me like royalty back there, and of course the reunion with Eileen was heartwarming. Boy, was she glad to see me. And me to see her again, of course. She actually thought I'd been snatched by dog snatchers and sold to some Middle-Eastern maharajah for big bucks."

Why a maharajah would pay big bucks for a dog that looks like a bat was frankly beyond me, but then Eileen Dobson was probably one of those pet parents that think their pet baby is the most beautiful and precious pet in all the world. Which, if you get right down to it, is what every pet parent thinks—and by extension every parent, period.

"Odelia had her baby," I said, filling Windex in on the latest from our home front.

"Oh, that's so great," said our canine friend. "Look, I'm sorry I couldn't come to the park last night, but I'm still settling in, and Eileen wouldn't have liked me wandering off in the middle of the night." She grimaced. "I guess she's afraid I'll disappear again."

"Totally understandable," I said.

"So where are you on the investigation?"

"Nowhere," I said honestly. "Plenty of suspects but nothing concrete."

"Too bad," she said. "Marsella deserves to be happy with Dewey, and as long as he's a suspect that's going to hang over them, won't it?"

"I'd totally forgotten that you know Marsella," I said.

"Oh, sure. She took such good care of me. And Shelley, too, of course."

"If Odelia would have kicked us out we had decided we wanted Shelley to adopt us," Dooley confessed.

"Who's this Shelley person?" asked Kingman.

"She volunteers at the shelter," I said. "Very sweet girl."

"I hope she and Gavin will finally be happy," said Windex.

"Shelley and Gavin? I didn't know those two were an item."

"Oh, absolutely. They're actually engaged, but don't tell anyone. It's a secret."

"Shelley is secretly engaged?" said Dooley excitedly. "That's so cool!"

"Why keep it a secret?" asked Kingman.

"Shelley's dad isn't too fond of Gavin," Windex revealed. "The Ecclestons are a very wealthy family."

"Cement, right?" I said.

"Yeah. And loaded. So Burke Eccleston, that's Shelley's dad, wants his little girl to marry someone with the same financial status, not the son of a local shoe salesman. Shelley introduced Gavin to him once and he told her not to let things get too serious. Said he didn't think he was the right boy for her. But she and Gavin are in love, and so they got engaged last month and are planning to elope and get married in the summer."

"That's so romantic!" said Dooley.

"How do you know so much about it?" asked Kingman.

"I lived at that shelter, remember?" said Windex with a smile. "And I overheard every single conversation Shelley and Gavin had. My heart really bled for them, and I hope they'll get their happy-ever-after at some point. Though if I understood correctly, the moment Shelley announces that she and Gavin are husband and wife, her dad will probably disown her and kick her out of the family firm, wanting nothing more to do with her. Which is so sad, really. But she doesn't care. She's going to marry Gavin anyway."

"Ooh, I hope they'll be together forever, and that one day her dad will realize what he's done and will beg her forgiveness and she will give it," said Dooley, the eternal romantic.

It was all food for thought, of course, and somehow it sparked an idea in my mind. It was a long shot, but at least it was something. And so I decided that when Odelia finally came home the next day, I'd tell her all about it so she could do some more digging.

I thanked Windex profusely, and the little doggie shrugged and said, "That's what friends are for, Max."

A warm glow spread out inside my chest. She was right. In the space of a few days, she'd gone from the devil's brood to being a dear friend. Odd how quickly things change.

CHAPTER 27

The next day, Odelia came home, and was greeted by her loving husband and four cats.

I have to be honest and say that the four of us were feeling the strain of uncertainty, and were not fully at ease.

"This is it, Max," said Brutus. "The moment of truth."

"We can always go and live with Shelley and Gavin," said Dooley. "Once they're married they'll want to share their home with us, I'm sure."

"It'll be fine," said Harriet. "It'll be just fine. Perfectly fine." But the oddly disconcerted look in her eyes told an entirely different story.

Odelia walked in, her baby in her arms, and was both surprised and touched by the warm welcome. In her absence, Tex and Chase and Uncle Alec had been messing around upstairs, turning the guest room into a nursery. It wasn't done yet, but Odelia was visibly pleased with this pleasant surprise. Though she did have one or two small amendments to make. The color of the walls, for one—she's not a fan of lime green in general—and the curtains—those heavy pea-green drapes weren't really suited for a nursery. But the baby's crib was fine, though it would have to move into the bedroom for now, of course. All in all, the room itself was okay, as a space, but all the rest pretty much had to go.

Chase bore her criticism with fortitude and promised to take her comments on board.

And then it was time to sit down as a family, and to start our new life. The four of us were still very much in a state of suspended animation, so to speak. And as Odelia took a seat at the kitchen counter, and started nursing her baby, it took her a while to notice that we were sitting on the floor, more or less patiently, and anxiously staring up at her.

"Hey, you guys," she said finally, after glancing in our direction once or twice. "Is everything all right?"

And then of course Dooley couldn't contain himself any longer. "Do we have to go and live with Shelley and Gavin now, Odelia, cause if we do, you have to tell us, since they're going off to get married soon, and might not be back for a while."

She frowned. "Now why in heaven's name would you go and live with Shelley and... Gavin, is it?"

Dooley nodded furiously. "Because Kingman said that babies and cats don't mix!"

"Oh, God, not with that old story again," said Odelia. "Look, I'm going to tell you one final time: nothing has changed. You're my cats and you'll always be my cats. And the fact that our family now consists of one extra member doesn't make any difference at all."

And to emphasize her words, just then the little one opened her mouth to give a loud sort of scream.

"Now now, Gracey," said Odelia soothingly. "Everything is all right, sweetie."

"Gracey?" asked Harriet. "Is that the baby's name?"

Too late, Odelia realized her faux-pas. She took it in stride. "I guess I might as well tell you. Max, Dooley, Harriet and Brutus—meet Grace Kingsley. Grace, meet my precious fur babies. They're the best friends any human could ever hope to meet."

Grace Kingsley took one good look at us and started screaming the house down.

At least now we knew: we were there to stay, no matter what Kingman said.

"There's something I need to tell you, Odelia," I announced quietly, once Grace had decided to settle down. And so I told her about the idea I'd had concerning the case.

"Are you sure?" she asked with a look of concern.

I nodded. "Pretty much. You'll have to check, of course."

"I will," she said, giving my words some further thought. "Oh, dear. If what you're saying is true, she'll be devastated."

"I know, but that can't be helped."

"No, of course not." She got up with some effort. "Well, I'll tell Chase and he can get the ball rolling."

"How do you want to play this?" I asked, watching with concern how she moved with some difficulty.

She gave me a smile. "I'll be fine, Max. In fact we'll all be fine now." She gave Grace a tender kiss on the chubby cheek. "Isn't that right, baby?"

She shouldn't have said that, of course, for Grace obviously was just like us: she didn't like to be disturbed when she was sleeping peacefully. Unlike us, though, she gave vent to her annoyance by opening her mouth and pretending to be a fire alarm.

The four of us quickly skedaddled, out through the pet flap and into the backyard.

Of all the contingencies we'd anticipated, the fact that we wouldn't be able to get any sleep was one I hadn't accounted for.

"I told you that babies can get pretty loud, Max," said

Dooley, who had of course foreseen this scenario. "They can get as loud as jumbo jets."

"For the hundredth time, Dooley," I said. "Babies are not jumbo jets."

"You could have fooled me," Brutus grumbled with a pained grimace.

"How something so small can make so much noise is a mystery to me," said Harriet.

Inside the house, Grace was still continuing her imitation of a fire drill, and making her mommy and daddy wonder if A) she didn't particularly like her parental unit, B) she had somewhere else to be or C) she was practicing to become the next Mariah Carey.

I had the impression they were secretly hoping for the latter, but fearing for the first. I could have put their minds at ease, though. Any baby would have been lucky to land a couple of parents like Odelia and Chase. And pretty soon she'd realize this and relax.

Or so I hoped.

CHAPTER 28

We were back at the shelter, paying a visit to the office where we found Marsella. Shelley and Gavin were also there, wondering what all the fuss was about, and we were all seated in the small office behind reception. It was Marsella's office, and the walls were bedecked with posters decrying people to take better care of their pets, and that 'A dog is for life, not just for Christmas,' something I think we could all wholeheartedly agree on, even though personally I would have replaced the word 'dog' with 'cat.'

There was a small desk and a table where a couple of people could sit, and where Marsella held her weekly staff meetings, even if her staff consisted of volunteers.

Marsella was seated at the head of the table, with Chase, Odelia, Shelley and Gavin distributed amongst the other seats.

Dooley and I had been relegated to the floor, but that wasn't a hardship, as we'd discovered a bowl with kibble, and were happily tucking in. I wasn't sure if it was dog kibble or cat kibble but then beggars can't be choosers. It tasted great all the same.

"So what's going on?" asked Marsella, leading the meeting—or so she thought.

"You're probably aware that we've been investigating the murders of two women," said Chase, opening proceedings. "Dotty Ludkin, also known as Dotty Berg, and Calista Burden, also known as Calista Dunne. Both women were strangled in their respective homes last week."

"Yes, of course," said Marsella. "But what does that have to do with me? I already told you that I never met either of these women, and I'm pretty sure Dewey didn't, either."

"Dewey told us that he hadn't met Dotty *recently*," Odelia clarified, putting the emphasis on the last word, causing Marsella to frown, "and now we think he was telling us the truth. You see, Dotty and Calista were involved in a scheme whereby they offered their services to take potential husbands for a test run, as they called it. Dotty would try to seduce them and if they failed, their clients would know they weren't marriage material. If they didn't fall for Dotty's charms, they could count themselves lucky."

"What a perverse setup," said Shelley. "I never heard of such a thing."

"Did a lot of women go for this arrangement?" asked Marsella.

"Yes, they did," said Odelia. "By all accounts Calista was very successful, and made a lot of money in a short amount of time. And so did Dotty. So much so that she told her boyfriend that soon she'd have enough money to buy an apartment or even a house."

"I can't imagine trying to trick your fiancé into that kind of thing," said Shelley.

"Yeah, me neither," said Marsella, though she appeared thoughtful now.

"Which brings us to you, Shelley," said Odelia, turning her

attention on the young volunteer. "We heard through the grapevine that you and Gavin are secretly engaged?"

Shelley's cheeks colored, and so did Gavin's. The young couple shared a look of confusion. "Who told you that?" Gavin demanded.

"Let's just say a reliable source," said Odelia, briefly glancing down at me.

"Is it true?" asked Chase. "Are you planning to elope and get married on the sly?"

"Well... yes," Shelley admitted, even as Gavin shook his head, clearly annoyed.

"You're getting married?" asked Marsella, who seemed completely surprised.

Shelley nodded. "I'm sorry I haven't told you, Marsella, but it was important for us that no one knew. Not even our best friends."

"But why elope?" asked Marsella. "I don't understand."

"It's my dad," said Shelley. "He has some very fixed ideas about the kind of husband I should marry."

"And I don't fit in with those ideas," said Gavin. "Not rich enough for his taste, I guess."

"Dad is afraid that I'll marry someone who's not in his class, whatever that means," said Shelley. "And when I introduced him to Gavin the first thing he said was, 'I hope you don't plan to marry that guy, honey. He's a frickin' shoe salesman for crying out loud.'"

"I'm not just *a* shoe salesman," said Gavin. "I stand to inherit my dad's business."

"Which is exactly what I told him, but he wasn't impressed."

"So you decided to elope and get married without your dad's permission," said Odelia.

Shelley nodded. "It seems like the best idea. He'll kick up a fuss, but there won't be anything he can do about it. By the time he finds out, it'll be too late." She gazed at her fiancé with loving eyes, and gave his hand a squeeze. "Won't be long now before I'll be Mrs. Gavin Blemish."

"The problem is that your dad must have realized how serious you were about Gavin," said Chase, "so he booked an interview with Calista Burden. Basically he asked her to set up a chance meeting between Gavin and Dotty, and see if she couldn't get him to fall for her charms. He gave them all the information he had on Gavin, which was extensive, since he'd also hired a private detective to find out as much as he could about Gavin's past, especially the girls he dated and his sexual preference, and relayed this information to Calista. Dotty took this information and used it to set a trap for Gavin."

Shelley's jaw had dropped, and she regarded her fiancé with consternation written all over her features. "No, she didn't. Gavin, tell me she didn't."

But Gavin had suddenly gone very still and quiet, and refused to meet Shelley's eyes.

"It pains me to say this, Shelley," said Odelia gently, "but I'm afraid the test was successful... from Calista and Dotty's perspective, at least—and your dad's, of course."

"You had a date with this woman?" Shelley demanded. "This-this prostitute?" Gavin's cheeks had flushed scarlet, extending both up and down his face. His ears were practically glowing, and he had bowed his head. His body language told us everything we needed to know, and Shelley cried, "Oh, my God, Gavin!"

"I'm sorry, all right!" the kid cried. "She was... very convincing."

"In Gavin's defense, Dotty made sure to transform herself so she looked exactly like the type of girl Gavin would fall for. She even made sure to get acquainted with some of his hobbies so she would be more convincing and have something to talk about."

"She said she was an animal rights activist," Gavin said quietly. "A true animal lover."

"Gavin!"

"I know, and I'm sorry!"

"I don't believe this," said Shelley. "And you're saying my dad set them up to this?"

"Yes, he did," said Odelia.

"But... why didn't he tell me about it? I mean, why didn't he gloat?"

"Because your dad got the message from Calista that Gavin had passed the test with flying colors. That not only didn't he fall for Dotty's charms but he told her he was in love with another girl and he planned to marry her and make her happy."

Shelley frowned. "I don't get it. Why would this Calista person do that?"

Odelia took a deep breath. "Because it wasn't Calista writing that message, but Gavin."

Shelley seemed confused for a moment, then finally understanding dawned. "No," she said in a low voice. "Oh, please God, no!"

"I'm afraid so," said Chase. "Once we suspected Gavin, we tracked his movements for that night. His dad told us he said he was going out to a club, and from that point it wasn't hard to reconstruct the events as they unfolded." He placed a series of pictures on the table in front of the young couple: a picture of Gavin and Dotty on the dance floor, one of them at the bar. A picture of the two of them walking along a street at night, and one in his car driving away. "Notice the time code," said Chase. "Ten forty-five on the night Dotty and Calista were both murdered. We also searched your apartment, Gavin, and found Dotty and

Calista's phones and laptops. So will you tell us what happened, exactly?"

Gavin, who'd hung his head, spoke haltingly, clearly deeply ashamed of what he'd done. "I left Dotty's apartment around midnight, but realized I'd left my phone so I went back to grab it. The door wasn't locked so I pushed it open. She was on the phone, reporting to her boss about how the night had gone. She said I'd fallen for her like a sucker, and how happy Burke would be with her work. Said I'd been the easiest mark she'd ever had and that fat bonus Burke had promised was theirs.

"So I confronted her, and she confessed that she was working for your father. That he was going to tell you everything. That they had pictures, video, the works, and that I was never going to see you again." He rubbed his cheek. "I don't know, I just suddenly saw red. I don't even remember what happened next, but when I came to my senses, she wasn't moving. She just lay there, staring up at me—dead. I just sat there for a while, realizing what I'd done, and thinking about what I needed to do to make sure this never came back to me. So I took her phone and checked it for the address of her boss. I drove over there and..." His voice faltered, and a tear slid down his cheek.

"It didn't hurt that you had some experience breaking into people's homes," Chase supplied. "I found a conviction for B&E in the distant past. Something I should have seen sooner, only you weren't on our radar then."

"I was a rebellious kid," said Gavin. "After my mom died I got involved with a pretty bad crowd. It drove my dad up the wall. But after I was caught and convicted I turned my life around. I never offended again."

"Until now with Dotty and Calista."

He nodded silently, ashamed to look his fiancée in the eye.

"So you broke into Calista's place, strangled her—"

Shelley released a moan that was a mixture of disbelief and hurt.

"—and sent that reassuring message to Shelley's dad, telling him the test had failed, and that as far as she was concerned you'd make a great addition to the family."

"Once I started down this road, I had no other choice but to finish it," said Gavin quietly. "Calista knew Dotty was with me. She'd have told the police and I'd be done for."

"How could you be sure that no one else knew about this?" asked Chase.

He shrugged. "I couldn't. But it stood to reason that if they used encrypted apps, the only people who knew would be Dotty and her boss. And besides, what other choice did I have at this point? I just had to hope and pray that no one else would find out."

"Unfortunately we did find out," said Odelia.

"But how?" asked the kid now, looking up at her. "I was so careful."

"I know you were, but clearly you weren't careful enough."

Shelley, who'd gone through different stages of shock, was now at the stage where she was slowly coming to terms with the fact that her fiancé hadn't merely cheated on her, but was also a double murderer.

"This doesn't have to change anything for us, Shel," the young man pleaded. "Okay, so I messed up, and I'm sorry, but I promise that Dotty didn't mean anything to me. It's you I love. You see, I was tricked. It was your dad who tricked me. I didn't stand a chance."

"Yes, you did," said Shelley. "You had a choice, Gavin. You always had a choice. And instead of choosing me, you chose Dotty."

"But I'm telling you, it was just a fling."

"You killed two women, Gavin!" She'd risen to her feet and stood, hands balled into fists. "You're a murderer! A killer!" And then she fled the room on a loud, desperate sob.

For a moment, no one spoke, then Chase said, "Gavin Blemish, I'm arresting you for the murders of Dotty Ludkin and Calista Burden."

"Oh, God, what have I done!" Gavin cried.

"Nothing good," Dooley murmured next to me.

CHAPTER 29

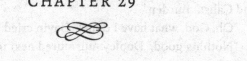

We were in Tex and Marge's backyard, enjoying a fine spread of delicious foods, as offered by the proud new grandparents. You could have called it a baby shower, but in actual fact it was our regular Saturday night barbecue, only with the addition of a new family member: Grace Kingsley.

"I wonder if Grace will be able to talk to us, too," said Dooley. The little one was tucked in bed, with a baby monitor in place in case she woke up. And if that wasn't enough, Odelia or Chase got up pretty much every five minutes to go and check on her.

"I hadn't actually thought of that," I admitted. "But I guess she will. She's a female descendent, so Odelia's gift will probably pass down to her."

"Oh, yay," said Harriet. "Finally a little princess who'll appreciate a fellow princess."

"How soon do you think she'll start talking?" asked Brutus.

"When do babies start talking?" I said. "I have no idea, actually."

"Odelia will know. She's been reading all those books," said Dooley.

"And watching all those documentaries," I added. And unfortunately we had to watch them along with her. Though since we'd slept through most of them, not much of the information had stuck with us.

"So you solved another case, didn't you, Maxie baby?" said Brutus, a touch of envy in his voice. "How do you do it? Case after case after case? I get tired just thinking about it."

"It's a knack," said Harriet. "Like some cats can jump very high, Max solves mysteries."

"It's because he has such a big brain," said Dooley proudly. "Someone should measure it, but I'll bet that Max's brain is probably as big as any human's. Or maybe even bigger."

"You should donate your brain to science, Max," said Brutus. "In fact you could donate it now. I'm sure those scientists will be very pleased."

Dooley frowned. "But how can Max donate his brain when he still needs it?" But then he got a bright idea. "Maybe he can loan it to science. Like, for a week or something? And then they can give it back."

"I'm afraid that once you donate your brain to science you don't get it back again, Dooley," I said, not too bothered by Brutus's barbs.

"What do you mean!" Dooley cried. "Those scientists have to give it back. Otherwise it's stealing!"

"You only donate your brain when you're dead, Dooley," said Harriet with an eye roll.

"Dead! But they can't make Max dead!"

"Nobody is going to make me dead," I assured him, and darted a look at Brutus to say, 'Now look what you've done.'

Brutus shrugged and displayed a small grin. "So tell us about your case, Max. I can see you're *dying* to."

"I'm not dying to tell you about my case, Brutus," I said.

"One thing isn't clear to me," said Harriet. "How did Shelley's dad find out about her secret engagement if they didn't tell anyone?"

"Yeah, he couldn't have heard it from Windex," said Brutus.

"Actually he heard it from the jeweler where the couple bought their engagement rings," I said. "The jeweler recognized Shelley and gave her dad a call. You see, Burke and the jeweler are both members of the Rotary Club, and the jeweler knew how particular Burke Eccleston was about his daughter's suitors, especially after Shelley's mom died a couple of years ago. So Burke hired a private eye to have Gavin investigated, and when he heard about Calista's unique service, figured it was the only way to convince Shelley that she was about to make a big mistake. And as it turns out, he was right, of course."

"Poor Shelley," said Dooley. "She looked so sad."

"She looked furious," I corrected him. "And I'm sure she'll land on her feet."

"Next time she gets engaged she'll be more careful, though," said Harriet. "She won't buy her engagement rings from one of her dad's friends."

"Or maybe next time she'll find a boyfriend her dad approves of," said Brutus.

"Whatever the case, I think it's safe to say that Shelley is better off without Gavin," I said. "If the guy saw red when Dotty revealed he'd been tricked, I can't imagine what he'd do when he got mad with Shelley at some point. He probably would have killed her, too."

"But they were so in love!" said Dooley.

"Couples rarely stay in love for perpetuity, Dooley," I said. "Relationships go through ups and downs, and if Gavin killed Dotty because she was going to mess up his relationship with Shelley, that doesn't bode well for the future. No, all things considered Burke Eccleston probably saved his daughter's life by his unusual initiative."

"I still think it's a pretty rotten thing to do," said Harriet. "Imagine if all dads hired a prostitute to 'test' their daughters' fiancés. It would be a pretty strange world."

We all looked at Tex, and I think we were wondering if he would have hired Calista to put Chase to the test before he gave his blessing for the cop's relationship with Odelia.

And our humans must have been thinking along the same lines, for at that moment Gran said, "When your daughter is of age, and she starts dating boys, are you going to hire a hooker to test them, Chase?" Judging from her mischievous grin she knew exactly how provocative her question was, but still decided to ask it.

"I doubt it," said Chase, with a quick glance to his wife. "When Grace comes home with a boy one day—far, far, *far* into the future—I intend to put the fear of God into him, and tell him I'll wring his pimply neck with my bare hands if he dares to hurt my little girl."

Uncle Alec grinned. "I think that should do the trick."

"I wish my dad had done the same for me," said Gran. "Then I wouldn't have been saddled with that no-good husband of mine."

"If you hadn't been saddled with that no-good husband of yours," said Marge, "then I wouldn't be here, and nor would Alec. And that means Odelia wouldn't be here either, or Grace."

"You have to take the good with the bad, honey," said Scarlett. "Such is life."

"Easy for you to say," Gran grumbled, and took a sniff from her lamb cutlet.

"Where's Dallas, by the way?" asked Marge. "I haven't seen him for a couple of days."

"Yeah, I kinda lost track of him," said Gran moodily.

"Talk of the devil," said Charlene, and gestured with her head to a man who'd just rounded the corner. It was of course Dallas de Pravé, Gran's Finnish billionaire. He was accompanied by a smallish man with spectacles, whom we'd never seen before.

"Greetings!" the smallish man said, making an all-encompassing gesture. "At this time Mr. de Pravé would like to say a few words."

"Who are you?" asked Gran, eyeing the man suspiciously.

"My name is Troy Packer, and I work for the Finnish Embassy as a translator," said the man. "Mr. de Pravé came to us this morning, and together we've come to the conclusion that there seems to be a misunderstanding."

"What misunderstanding?" asked Gran. Then her face fell. "Don't tell me he's gay."

"Mr. de Pravé isn't gay, but Mr. de Pravé is very impatient to discover why you have been waiting so long to show him your muffin maker."

Gran blushed scarlet at this. "Do we really have to do this in front of my entire family?"

"If you don't mind," said Troy.

"Oh, very well then," said Gran. "Tell him I haven't shown him my muffin maker because he hasn't shown me his sausage maker. And it's not for lack of trying on my part. I've tried to kiss him plenty of times, but he doesn't seem interested."

"I don't understand," said Troy, displaying a confused frown.

"Look, I'm a simple woman," said Gran. "No sausage, no muffin. All clear now?"

"But... Mr. de Pravé doesn't make sausages. Mr. de Pravé owns a chain of bakeries."

"Be that as it may, I have my standards," said Gran stubbornly. "I don't put out if he doesn't put out. Fair is fair."

Dallas de Pravé now burst forth into speech, producing a flow of words that was frankly impressive, seeing as we'd hardly heard his voice in all the time he'd been with us.

Troy nodded a few times very gravely, then said, "Mr. de Pravé says that he's still very interested in visiting your muffin factory, but unfortunately it would have to be now. He has an important engagement coming up and will have to leave for Finland tomorrow."

Gran's flushed face had turned even darker. "He wants to see my muffin... now?!"

"Yes, I'm afraid so," said Troy with a courteous bow. "As you Americans like to say: it's now or never." He flashed a most toothy grin. "So please show us your muffin, madam!"

"Well, of all the damn cheek!" Gran cried.

The loud and resounding report of two slaps echoed through the air, and for a moment all was quiet. Two men stood rubbing injured cheeks, and massaging hurt egos, then Dallas once more erupted into a stream of words, this time accompanied by a lot of angry gestures and even angrier looks thrown in Gran's direction.

"Mr. de Pravé would like you to know that he has no more interest in your muffins," said Troy sadly. "And also he demands an apology. When you told him aboard the cruise vessel that you owned a company called Vesta Muffin and subsequently invited him over for a visit, he took your word for it that you wanted to go into business together. Now he's not so sure."

"I don't own a muffin company," said Gran. "My *name* is Vesta Muffin."

As Troy translated these words, the rest of the family broke into soft titters of amusement. Finally Dallas stood nodding as he listened carefully, then flashed a smile.

"So you mean to say you don't want to sell your muffins to Mr. de Pravé?" asked Troy, just to be sure.

"After the horrible things he just said to me? Absolutely not!" said Gran. "Tell him loud and clear so there is no mistake: no more muffins! This shop is closed for business!"

"But Gran," said Odelia. "That man thought you owned a muffin factory. All he wanted was to buy your muffins and sell them in his chain of bakeries back home in Finland."

"Well, he blew his chance now, didn't he?" Gran fumed. "With his indecent proposals."

"But Vesta," said Chase. "Don't you see? It's all been one big misunderstanding!"

"I'll bet it has. I thought I finally found a decent billionaire and it turns out he's a pervert and a lecher! And me, a great-grandmother!"

"I like muffins," said Charlene with a grin. "Very tasty."

"Oh, don't you muffin me, young lady," said Gran.

Troy had continued to translate, and Dallas now seemed to have understood all, for he stood laughing with distinct relish, his stocky frame shaking with honest mirth.

"Very funny!" he cried, wagging his finger in Gran's face.

"Well, I don't think it's funny at all," said Gran. She turned to Chase. "Can't you arrest him for indecent exposure or something?"

But before Chase could respond, Dallas had grabbed Gran's hand and pressed a most gallant kiss on it. Then he smiled at her and said, "I like American Muffin!" And then he was off, Troy Packer in his wake. And as they walked away, stage left, they were both laughing heartily.

"What an idiot," Gran muttered, then sighed. "And he seemed so promising."

"At least he said he likes you," said Scarlett, patting her hand consolingly.

"Yeah, Ma," said Uncle Alec. "He said he likes your muffins. What more do you want?"

"What are they talking about, Max?" asked Dooley. "What's all this stuff about Gran's muffins?"

"I'll explain to you later, Dooley," I told him.

"When, Max?"

I thought for a moment. "When Grace is old enough to understand."

"Oh, okay," he said. And lay down his head and went to sleep.

So easy. Maybe from now on I'd use that line more often. After all, it would be years before Grace reached that age when she started asking the difficult questions. The kind of questions Dooley always asked. Years and years and years.

Then again, maybe not. She was, after all, Odelia's daughter, Marge's granddaughter and Gran's great-granddaughter. Which meant we were in for some interesting times.

THE END

Thanks for reading! If you want to know when a new Nic Saint book comes out, sign up for Nic's mailing list: nicsaint.com/news

EXCERPT FROM PURRFECT MESS
(MAX 50)

Chapter One

"Max?"

"Mh?"

"Do you think James Bond could be played by a cat?"

It was one of those questions that makes you think, and so think is what I did. "What brought this on?" I said in an attempt at prevarication.

"Chase said that they're looking for a new actor to play James Bond, since the previous one feels he's too old for the role, and Odelia said they might pick a woman this time. So I was wondering why not a cat, you know?"

"I like your thinking, Dooley," I said. "Why not a cat indeed?"

"I mean, the time that only middle-aged white males could play James Bond is well and truly behind us. And to appeal to a larger demographic they should consider their options. And everybody likes cats, so they've got that pre-existing audience."

"I couldn't agree more," I said. We'd only recently

watched a James Bond movie on television, all of us cozily ensconced in the living room, the humans riveted to their TV set, and us cats wondering what all the fuss was about as usual. "Though it might be hard to find a cat that fits the part," I said, my thought processes a little sluggish on this, a lazy Saturday morning in the Kingsley home.

Dooley and I were in the backyard, enjoying those first few rays that do so much to warm up one's bones, the dewy grass nice and cool against my belly. Our humans—Odelia and Chase—were still in bed, and so was baby Grace, the latest addition to the clan.

"Brutus could do it," said Dooley. "He'd be perfect for the role."

"You're forgetting one thing, my friend," I said. "James Bond has a license to kill, and to do that he needs to be able to handle a gun, and since cats aren't naturally equipped by an otherwise wise and benevolent creator to handle a firearm, I think Brutus would be dropped from the lineup at his first audition. In fact he probably wouldn't even make it past the first selection."

This was enough to give my best friend pause. At least for a few minutes. But then he rallied. "Maybe they can adopt a strict no-gun policy? Brutus could use his claws when he's under attack. I'll bet he can be equally lethal—or even more so—with his claws than by using a gun. He could be the new gun-less Bond."

"True, true," I admitted. Though frankly I had a feeling the James Bond aficionados might not agree if after sixty years the famous franchise suddenly went firearm-free. Then again, the question was probably moot, since as far as I knew, Brutus had never expressed an interest in being the next Bond.

"I bet they'll cast a dog," Dooley said moodily. "They always do."

"A dog would make a great spy," I said, trying to cheer him up. "Dogs are very photogenic. And popular, too. I'll bet if the next Bond was a dog it would be a big hit."

"Who would be a hit?" suddenly asked a voice in my rear.

It was, of course, our friend Harriet. She and her boyfriend Brutus now came sashaying in our direction, straight from the rose bushes where they like to spend some quality time of a morning—or an afternoon or even a night.

"The new James Bond," said Dooley without looking up. "They're casting a dog."

"A dog!" said Brutus. "You're not serious."

"Dooley is simply speculating," I hastened to say.

"Isn't that just typical?" Harriet scoffed. "It's always the same pets who have all the luck. I'm telling you, it's a dog's world out there, and us cats are always picked last."

"Dooley was just saying how you'd make the perfect Bond," I said, trying to interject a modicum of optimism and cheerfulness into the conversation.

"I know," said Harriet, simpering a little.

"No, I actually meant Bru—"

"I'd make some changes, of course," she blithely went on. "For one thing I'd make sure they drop that dreadfully dreary color scheme." She sighed excitedly. "I'm seeing lots of pinks and yellows. Maybe even some powder blue. And of course only happy faces from now on. Happy happy happy. And maybe we could do a big dance number to open the movie, with lots and lots of showcats, like in *La La Land*." She gave her partner a coy look. "My name is Bond. Harriet Bond."

"Excellent," Brutus murmured, though I could tell he wasn't as happy as he could have been at this example of creative casting. And you have to admit: Brutus Bond does have a nice ring to it. Better than Max Bond at any rate. Or even Dooley Bond.

Then again, it was no use speculating, since no Bond

EXCERPT FROM PURRFECT MESS (MAX 50)

producer in their right mind would ever cast a cat in the coveted role of Ian Fleming's famous secret agent. Cats are simply too cute. And a cute Bond is a big no-no. And so instead of thinking of ways and means of saving the planet from a dastardly evil genius and his henchmen, Harriet joined us on the lawn, and let the sunlight play about her noble visage.

Brutus, meanwhile, ventured into the house to subject his food bowl to a spot check, and as the birds tweeted in a nearby tree, and a neighbor took his lawnmower for a test run, I soon found myself drifting off to sleep. And I probably would have dreamt of Bond girls and fancy cars and nifty spy gadgetry if not suddenly a fire engine started screaming nearby.

We were wide awake within milliseconds, and it took me a while to realize it wasn't a fire that was about to consume some innocent home, but baby Grace who had decided that she required nourishment and she required it right now!

"Oh, dear," said Harriet, once she had her heartbeat under control again. "I don't think I'll ever get used to that terrible sound."

I could have told her that if she was going to be the next James Bond, there probably were worse things she needed to tackle than the sound of a hungry infant, but I wisely kept my tongue.

We all directed a curious look at the upstairs window, behind which I could easily picture the homely scene that was now playing out: Chase and Odelia would have immediately woken up, and were presumably staggering, still sleep drunk, in the direction of the cradle that housed the source of all this clamor. Moments later, the screaming stopped, and we all shared a look of satisfaction. Odelia had done it again: she'd managed to tame the savage beast that lurks behind the pure face of innocence.

EXCERPT FROM PURRFECT MESS (MAX 50)

"Who knew that such a tiny human could produce such a big sound?" said Harriet, shaking her head in wonder.

"She'll have a great career as an opera singer," said Dooley. "She already has the volume, now all she has to do is work on expanding her repertoire."

He was right. So far Grace's performances kept within the one-note range.

From next door, Fifi came trotting up. Fifi is a Yorkshire Terrier, and probably one of the nicest dogs alive—and I don't say this lightly, as everyone knows that most dogs are foul creatures who like nothing better than to chase cats up trees.

"Kurt isn't happy, you guys," she said as she joined us.

"Kurt is never happy," I said. Kurt is Fifi's human, and our perpetually grumpy next-door neighbor. Though what he isn't happy about tends to vary day by day.

"What isn't he happy about this time?" asked Brutus, popping out through the pet flap, satisfied that his bowl still contained the necessary foodstuffs.

"It's the baby," said Fifi. "He says she's way too loud, and if this keeps up he's going to file a noise complaint."

"Good luck with that," said Brutus. "Doesn't he know Grace's dad is a cop?"

"Oh, he knows, which is why he won't file the complaint in Hampton Cove. He's going straight to the top."

"The top?" I asked, intrigued. "You mean the Mayor?"

"The Governor," said Fifi. "He's going to claim that his rights as a citizen and a taxpayer are being trampled on. And he says there's a precedent."

"What precedent?"

"Remember how they wanted to build an airport in Happy Bays last year and how the neighbors successfully petitioned against it? Well, he says the same principle applies."

I have to confess we were all a little flabbergasted, but finally I pointed out, "A baby isn't an airplane, Fifi."

"Max is absolutely right," Dooley chimed in. "For one thing, babies don't fly." He turned to me. "Do they?"

"No, Dooley," I said. "Babies don't fly."

"Unlike the storks that deliver them," said Dooley with a nod in my direction.

"I know that," said Fifi, "and Kurt knows that, but he says she makes the same noise as a jumbo jet, and since he was here first, that dreadful baby has to go. And if the Governor doesn't get rid of her, he's taking his case up to the President."

"Dreadful baby?" said Harriet. "Did he really call Grace a dreadful baby?"

"Actually he used a much stronger term," said Fifi with a touch of bashfulness. "But I don't want to be rude."

"Kurt isn't a very nice person," said Dooley.

"He's nice to me," said Fifi. "But you're right. He's not very nice to other people."

"And babies," said Dooley.

"Babies are people, too, Dooley," said Harriet. "Only they're a lot smaller."

"They're like miniature people," Brutus explained with an indulgent smile. "They have tiny toes and tiny fingers and tiny ears and a tiny nose and—"

"Yes, yes, we get the picture," I interrupted my friend's vivid word picture of what, exactly, constitutes a human baby.

"They're not really going to get rid of Grace, are they, Max?" said Dooley, a look of concern now marring my friend's funny little face.

"Of course not," I said. "The whole idea is ridiculous."

Still, I have to admit I wasn't sanguine about Fifi's report, straight from the front lines. Kurt has been known to throw the odd shoe in our direction, you see, expressing in word and gesture his displeasure with our vocal performance of an evening. Was it so hard to imagine the lengths he'd go to to rid himself of an admittedly vociferous infant? After all, no man is born a shoe thrower. As a young boy Kurt probably threw matches at passing cats, then gradually worked his way up to twigs and sticks, then shoes, and now he was moving into the baby removal business. If he kept this up, pretty soon he'd morph into a full-fledged Bond villain and construct a secret lair underneath his lawn so he could destroy the world.

Chapter Two

Vesta Muffin hadn't slept well. Now she'd read in some magazine that once you reach a certain age you need less shut-eye but lately she'd been more awake than asleep during those restless nights. It had become so bad she'd developed a habit of getting up in the middle of the night and going for a midnight walk around the block. The fresh air and the brisk exercise usually tired her out to such an extent that by the time she tumbled into bed again, she slept like the proverbial baby... until what seemed like moments later it was time to start her day.

She'd talked to Tex, her son-in-law, who was a doctor and was supposed to know about this stuff, but he'd merely offered her some platitudes about old age that she hadn't appreciated in the least.

"Old age, my foot," she now muttered as she threw off the comforter and swung her feet to the floor. Once again she felt she hadn't enjoyed nearly enough sleep, and feared that if this kept up, she might even develop issues with her ticker. Hadn't she read somewhere that insomnia could lead to heart problems?

EXCERPT FROM PURRFECT MESS (MAX 50)

"Chamomile tea," her daughter Marge had advised. "And no screens before bedtime."

"I hate tea, and I never had trouble falling asleep after watching TV before."

"I'm not talking about TV, Ma. I'm talking about your phone."

"My phone? What's wrong with my phone?"

"Blue light," Marge had said, rather mysteriously, she thought.

"Blue light, my ass," she said as she threw her curtains wide to see what the weather was like. The sun was benevolently splashing its rays across a grateful world, but Vesta squinted, giving it the evil eye. "Sunlight, that's the problem," she said. Maybe she had to move up North, where they never had any light, blue or otherwise. Wasn't there some place in Alaska where they never got any light at all? Months and months of utter and complete darkness? Now that would probably lull her to sleep—a nice long winter sleep. Like a bear. Or a hedgehog. Then again, since she hated the cold, that probably wasn't an option either.

She sighed deeply and shuffled out of her room and into the bathroom, which, lucky for her, hadn't yet been occupied by the rest of the household. With a flick of the wrist, she locked the door, and started the tedious daily ritual of addressing her personal hygiene needs—which were plenty and getting greater every day.

🐾

Tex awoke with a start, lifting his head half an inch from the pillow then letting it fall back again with a groan of dismay. It was his fervent wish that one morning he'd be able to get up before his mother-in-law, so he could be the first one to occupy the bathroom, but so far he hadn't yet succeeded in fulfilling this modest desire.

"We should have built a second bathroom," he now told his wife, who was stirring next to him.

"We still could," she muttered, her eyes firmly closed.

"But where? There's no space for a second bathroom."

"We could build one in the garden house," Marge suggested.

He gave this some thought. It was an idea, of course. When they'd recently rebuilt the house, he'd suggested to the architect to squeeze in a second bathroom, but the man had convinced them it wasn't feasible, nor was it necessary, since they were only three occupants. He'd pointed out that the man had never lived under the same roof as his mother-in-law, and the architect had given him a look of such compassion he'd been moved to tears and had never mentioned the topic again.

"We'll never get permission," he said as he rubbed the sleep from his eyes.

"We could build it illegally," said Marge.

He directed an indulgent smile at his wife of twenty-five years. "We're talking major plumbing, honey. No plumber would touch the project without the necessary permits."

Marge yawned and stretched, then gave him a yearning look. "For once in my life I want to be the first to get into the bathroom, Tex. The first one to take a shower."

"I know," he said. "Me, too." He sighed a wistful sigh. "But as I get older I'm starting to realize it's simply not in the cards for us. One of those pipe dreams like winning the lottery or finishing the crossword puzzle. We've been getting up earlier and earlier and she's still beating us to it. The woman never sleeps."

"And spends what seems like hours in there."

"Worse than Odelia when she was a teenager."

EXCERPT FROM PURRFECT MESS (MAX 50)

For a moment they both were silent as they contemplated ways and means of fixing a problem that had been vexing them since they'd invited Marge's mom to share their home with them. "We could always hire one of those cowboy builders," Marge suggested.

"You mean like the ones that destroyed our old home? Aren't they in jail?"

"There must be others," said Marge with a touch of desperation. "Others like them?"

He swallowed away a lump of unease. It was one thing to dream of going down a certain route, but quite another to actually go ahead and venture into illegality. Theirs had been a life built on a strict adherence to the rule of law. He never even jaywalked, and always dropped his litter in the appropriate receptacle. So the prospect of suddenly venturing into a life of crime gave him quite a jolt.

He blinked. "Are you sure about this?" he asked, his voice a little hoarse as he nervously licked his lips.

The voice of Marge's mother suddenly rang out. She'd burst into song and was obviously taking one of those long, hot showers she loved so much, using up all the hot water and leaving nothing for the rest of the family. *"I'm a poor, lonesome cowboy!"* she was belting at the top of her voice. *"And I'm a long way from home!"*

Marge hesitated but for a moment, then nodded eagerly. "Let's do it," she whispered.

In spite of his misgivings, he whispered back, "Don't tell your mother?"

Marge mimicked locking her lips and throwing away the key. "Cross my heart."

"And hope to die," he murmured. "Though on second thought, maybe scratch that."

"Let's break the law, Clyde," Marge smiled.

"Let's build ourselves an illegal bathroom, Bonnie," he smiled back.

And so it was decided. After walking the straight and narrow for forty-eight years—well, maybe forty-seven, since the first year of their lives they admittedly hadn't done a lot of walking—Tex and Marge Poole were embracing the life of crime—and the pitfalls of DIY plumbing.

Chapter Three

Grace had been washed and fed and was sleeping peacefully in her crib, and so Odelia sighed with relief as she nursed her cup of tea and took a breather at the kitchen counter. Chase had left for work and the house was suddenly very quiet, which was exactly the way she liked it. The cats were outside, escaping the din and hubbub a newborn baby inevitably brings, and since she was on maternity leave from work, frankly she had nothing to do and nothing to occupy her time but to take care of Grace.

She idly flipped through a few of the updates her boss had posted on the *Gazette* website and found herself reading some of the articles her replacement had written with a critical eye. Then, realizing how silly she was being, she put down the phone and suddenly found herself wondering what she would do for the rest of the day.

Having spent all of her adult life occupied in gainful employment, this sudden lull in what otherwise was a modestly stellar career was a little disconcerting to say the least. Dan had told her to take it easy for a while, and not to spend even one second thinking about the job. And Chase had told her that from now on she wasn't to even contemplate assisting him in his own job—no running around fighting crime with a baby tucked in her arms!—and even her uncle had said that her days of gleefully hobnobbing with

EXCERPT FROM PURRFECT MESS (MAX 50)

notorious killers and other scum of the Hampton Cove underworld were finally over—and not a moment too soon!

But if she wasn't a reporter, and she wasn't a detective, then what was she?

Grace made a slight gurgling sound in her sleep and Odelia smiled. First and foremost, of course, she was a mother, and maybe that was enough. At least for now.

She did wonder how her cats felt about this whole transition to a more peaceful and uneventful life. Max had assisted her and Chase so many times in collaring criminals and identifying villains that he must be experiencing withdrawal symptoms. Though to be honest he seemed perfectly happy with this new phase in their lives. Content, even.

Just then, her phone vibrated and she immediately picked up, darting a quick glance to Grace. She lowered her voice, not wanting to wake up the baby and said, "Yes, Odelia Kingsley speaking?"

It was an unknown number, and even though she probably should adopt Gran's stance on unknown callers: namely, to ignore them and when they don't leave a message report them to your provider and then block them, she simply couldn't. On your true reporter, worth their salt, a call from an unknown number acts very much like the proverbial red flag to a bull: it heats up the blood and makes their nerve endings sizzle with anticipatory excitement. For who knows, it could be the President, offering an exclusive sit-down to discuss their latest brainwave. Or Adele, suggesting a duet for her next album '35,' or Kim Kardashian, offering a part in her new reality show. Or it could even be a publisher suggesting they publish her autobiography. A girl can only dream!

"Hey, Odelia," the voice on the other end spoke. "It's Tessa. Is this a bad time?"

She gulped a little, then managed, "Oh, hey, Tessa!"

She'd met Tessa Torrance and her husband Prince Dante in England a while back, when the couple had been relentlessly hounded by the tabloids and eventually driven out of the country by those rabid newshounds.

"I'm sorry to drop this on you," said Tessa, "but I'm afraid I need a favor. Again."

"Absolutely," she said immediately. "Anything."

"The thing is... a dear, dear friend of ours finds himself in something of a pickle. And so I was wondering if you could help him out. I wouldn't be asking you this," she hastened to add, "if it wasn't extremely important. You see, he urgently needs a place to lie low for a while, a place where no one would think to look for him. In other words: Hampton Cove."

"Of course," she said, blinking a few times at this unexpected request. Then she produced what she hoped was a sufficiently airy chuckle. "He's not a fugitive from justice, is he? Cause I'm not sure Chase would approve if we were harboring a known criminal."

For a moment Tessa didn't speak, and Odelia's cheeks colored. Then her friend said, "I'm afraid you're going to have to trust me on this, Odelia."

So this man *was* a criminal! Oh, dear.

"So can I tell him to head to your place?"

"Um..."

"I would host him myself but you know how I'm constantly under surveillance by some of the same paps that drove us out of England. Can you believe they're using drones now, trying to snap a shot of us walking in our own backyard?"

She murmured a sound of commiseration, even as she wondered how she was going to explain to Chase that she had agreed to supply room and board to some British crook.

EXCERPT FROM PURRFECT MESS (MAX 50)

"He hasn't... *murdered* anyone, has he?" she finally insisted.

This time it was Tessa's turn to produce a light chuckle. "No, Odelia. He's not a murderer. But he is in big trouble, and I can't thank you and Chase enough for doing this."

"So—"

"Okay, I gotta go. Dante is calling me. Toodle-pip, honey. And thanks again."

"But I—" But the Duchess of Essex was gone and she found herself staring at her phone in mild horror. Chase was going to be very unhappy when he discovered what she'd let herself in for this time. At least the man—whoever he was—hadn't murdered anyone, which was a small consolation.

She chewed her bottom lip as she wondered where they were going to put this mystery guest. They'd turned the guest room into a nursery, so that was out of the question. And she couldn't very well ask Tessa's friend to sleep on the couch. And so it was with a groan of dismay that she finally picked up her phone again.

"Mom?" she said as the call connected. "Help!"

ABOUT NIC

Nic has a background in political science and before being struck by the writing bug worked odd jobs around the world (including but not limited to massage therapist in Mexico, gardener in Italy, restaurant manager in India, and Berlitz teacher in Belgium).

When he's not writing he enjoys curling up with a good (comic) book, watching British crime dramas, French comedies or Nancy Meyers movies, sampling pastry (apple cake!), pasta and chocolate (preferably the dark variety), twisting himself into a pretzel doing morning yoga, going for a run, and spoiling his big red tomcat Tommy.

He lives with his wife (and aforementioned cat) in a small village smack dab in the middle of absolutely nowhere and is probably writing his next 'Mysteries of Max' book right now.

www.nicsaint.com

ALSO BY NIC SAINT

The Mysteries of Max
Purrfect Murder
Purrfectly Deadly
Purrfect Revenge
Purrfect Heat
Purrfect Crime
Purrfect Rivalry
Purrfect Peril
Purrfect Secret
Purrfect Alibi
Purrfect Obsession
Purrfect Betrayal
Purrfectly Clueless
Purrfectly Royal
Purrfect Cut
Purrfect Trap
Purrfectly Hidden
Purrfect Kill
Purrfect Boy Toy
Purrfectly Dogged
Purrfectly Dead
Purrfect Saint
Purrfect Advice
Purrfect Passion

A Purrfect Gnomeful
Purrfect Cover
Purrfect Patsy
Purrfect Son
Purrfect Fool
Purrfect Fitness
Purrfect Setup
Purrfect Sidekick
Purrfect Deceit
Purrfect Ruse
Purrfect Swing
Purrfect Cruise
Purrfect Harmony
Purrfect Sparkle
Purrfect Cure
Purrfect Cheat
Purrfect Catch
Purrfect Design
Purrfect Life
Purrfect Thief
Purrfect Crust
Purrfect Bachelor
Purrfect Double
Purrfect Date
Purrfect Hit
Purrfect Baby
Purrfect Mess

The Mysteries of Max Box Sets

Box Set 1 (Books 1-3)
Box Set 2 (Books 4-6)
Box Set 3 (Books 7-9)
Box Set 4 (Books 10-12)
Box Set 5 (Books 13-15)
Box Set 6 (Books 16-18)
Box Set 7 (Books 19-21)
Box Set 8 (Books 22-24)
Box Set 9 (Books 25-27)
Box Set 10 (Books 28-30)
Box Set 11 (Books 31-33)
Box Set 12 (Books 34-36)
Box Set 13 (Books 37-39)
Box Set 14 (Books 40-42)
Box Set 15 (Books 43-45)
Box Set 16 (Books 46-48)

The Mysteries of Max Big Box Sets

Big Box Set 1 (Books 1-10)
Big Box Set 2 (Books 11-20)

The Mysteries of Max Shorts

Purrfect Santa (3 shorts in one)
Purrfectly Flealess
Purrfect Wedding

Nora Steel

Murder Retreat

The Kellys

Murder Motel

Death in Suburbia

Emily Stone

Murder at the Art Class

Washington & Jefferson

First Shot

Alice Whitehouse

Spooky Times

Spooky Trills

Spooky End

Spooky Spells

Ghosts of London

Between a Ghost and a Spooky Place

Public Ghost Number One

Ghost Save the Queen

Box Set 1 (Books 1-3)

A Tale of Two Harrys

Ghost of Girlband Past

Ghostlier Things

Charleneland

Deadly Ride

Final Ride

Neighborhood Witch Committee

Witchy Start

Witchy Worries

Witchy Wishes

Saffron Diffley

Crime and Retribution

Vice and Verdict

Felonies and Penalties (Saffron Diffley Short 1)

The B-Team

Once Upon a Spy

Tate-à-Tate

Enemy of the Tates

Ghosts vs. Spies

The Ghost Who Came in from the Cold

Witchy Fingers

Witchy Trouble

Witchy Hexations

Witchy Possessions

Witchy Riches

Box Set 1 (Books 1-4)

The Mysteries of Bell & Whitehouse

One Spoonful of Trouble

Two Scoops of Murder

Three Shots of Disaster

Box Set 1 (Books 1-3)

A Twist of Wraith

A Touch of Ghost

A Clash of Spooks

Box Set 2 (Books 4-6)
The Stuffing of Nightmares
A Breath of Dead Air
An Act of Hodd
Box Set 3 (Books 7-9)
A Game of Dons

Standalone Novels
When in Bruges
The Whiskered Spy

ThrillFix
Homejacking
The Eighth Billionaire
The Wrong Woman

CPSIA information can be obtained
at www.ICGtesting.com
Printed in the USA
LVHW031218210423
744984LV00004B/384

9 789464 446487